Praise for *New Yor[...]*
bestselling a[...]

"Forget the hot chocolat[...]
heater—Tawny Weber's [...]
you plenty warm this season."

—*USA TODAY*

"Fiery hot sex scenes, strong characters and exciting action make this one of the best stories in the Uniformly Hot! miniseries—and one of the best Blaze reads."

—*RT Book Reviews* on
A SEAL's Seduction

"A fun, sexy tale that will have you laughing at Eden's antics as well as fantasizing about what it would be like to have Cade all to yourself, *A SEAL's Surrender* is a sizzling hit."

—*Romance Reviews Today*

"*A SEAL's Salvation* is a new selection in the Uniformly Hot! miniseries and earns its place there with sizzlling sex scenes, a blazing hot bad boy turned decorated hero, and a heroine who finds her own strength while helping our troubled alpha."

—*Night Owl Reviews*

"Blistering hot, *Sex, Lies and Valentines*...is a witty, sensual contemporary romantic suspense that readers will find impossible to put down until they reach the delightful ending."

—*Romance Junkies*

"Tawny Weber certainly knows how to pen delicious stories, filled with heat, humour and lovable characters. *Sex, Lies and Midnight* proves again that you cannot go wrong with a Tawny Weber tale."

—*CataRomance*

Dear Reader,

I love the holidays, so it was extra fun to visit a few of them in this story, beginning with Halloween. It just seemed right that we kick off with treat time! And boy, oh boy, is Mitch Donovan a treat. I adore these sexy SEALs and Mitch's new-kid-on-the-block status with the team makes him even more interesting to get to know. Especially for Livi Kane, aka The Body Babe. Who better for a military machine than a fitness queen?

One of the benefits of writing this book was it inspired a great need to exercise! I'm fond of fitness as a rule, but tend to keep it on the as-I-get-to-it level. But Livi's approach is stuck in my head now so I might have to step up my game. Of course, it'd be easier with a great fitness instructor leading the way, right?

As fitting for the most romantic month of the year, my favorite scene in the story takes place on Valentine's Day. I hope your Valentine's Day is a fabulous one, and that you enjoy Livi and Mitch's journey through their holidays.

And if you're on the web, I'll be sharing Livi's pasta recipe on my website, and insider peeks into this story and others. Stop by my website at tawnyweber.com or find me on Facebook at facebook.com/tawnyweber.romanceauthor.

Happy reading!

Tawny Weber

Paper back WEBER

505830 c.l #5.50

Brodart 1-20-15

Tawny Weber

—

A SEAL's Secret

PROPERTY OF
EGF CAMPBELL LIBRARY

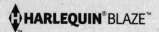

HARLEQUIN® BLAZE™

If you purchased this book without a cover you should be aware
that this book is stolen property. It was reported as "unsold and
destroyed" to the publisher, and neither the author nor the
publisher has received any payment for this "stripped book."

Recycling programs
for this product may
not exist in your area.

ISBN-13: 978-0-373-79835-3

A SEAL's Secret

Copyright © 2015 by Tawny Weber

All rights reserved. Except for use in any review, the reproduction or
utilization of this work in whole or in part in any form by any electronic,
mechanical or other means, now known or hereinafter invented, including
xerography, photocopying and recording, or in any information storage
or retrieval system, is forbidden without the written permission of the
publisher, Harlequin Enterprises Limited, 225 Duncan Mill Road,
Don Mills, Ontario M3B 3K9, Canada.

This is a work of fiction. Names, characters, places and incidents are
either the product of the author's imagination or are used fictitiously,
and any resemblance to actual persons, living or dead, business
establishments, events or locales is entirely coincidental.

This edition published by arrangement with Harlequin Books S.A.

For questions and comments about the quality of this book,
please contact us at CustomerService@Harlequin.com.

® and TM are trademarks of Harlequin Enterprises Limited or its
corporate affiliates. Trademarks indicated with ® are registered in the
United States Patent and Trademark Office, the Canadian Intellectual
Property Office and in other countries.

Printed in U.S.A.

A *New York Times* and *USA TODAY* bestselling author of over thirty hot books, **Tawny Weber** has been writing sassy, sexy romances since her first Harlequin Blaze book was published in 2007. A fan of Johnny Depp, cupcakes and color coordination, she spends a lot of her time shopping for cute shoes, scrapbooking and hanging out on Facebook.

Readers can check out Tawny's books at her website, tawnyweber.com, or join her Red Hot Readers Club for goodies like free reads, complete first-chapter excerpts, recipes, insider story info and much more. Look for her on Facebook at facebook.com/tawnyweber.romanceauthor.

Books by Tawny Weber
HARLEQUIN BLAZE

Just for the Night
Sex, Lies and Mistletoe
Sex, Lies and Midnight
Blazing Bedtime Stories, Volume VII
"Wild Thing"
Nice & Naughty
A SEAL's Seduction
A SEAL's Surrender
Midnight Special
Naughty Christmas Nights
A SEAL's Salvation
A SEAL's Kiss
A SEAL's Fantasy
Christmas with a SEAL

COSMOPOLITAN RED-HOT READS FROM HARLEQUIN
Fearless

Visit the Author Profile page
at Harlequin.com for more titles

To Melyssa with big hugs and so much love!

Thank you for naming Morgan.

1

Halloween

"My, oh, my, talk about temptation. A room filled with sexy sailors, an abundance of alcohol and deliciously fattening food."

Olivia Kane cast an appreciative look around Olive Oyl's, the posh yet funky bar that catered to the local naval base and locals alike. She loved the view of the various temptations, even though she knew she wouldn't be indulging in any.

Not that she didn't want to.

She'd love nothing more than to dive into a forty-ounce margarita and chow down on a plate of fully loaded nachos. But her career hinged on her body being in prime condition, so she'd long ago learned to resist empty calories.

And the sexy sailors?

One of those, she wouldn't mind indulging in. Livi barely kept from pouting. She was pretty sure a wild bout with a yummy military hunk would do amazing things for her body, too.

It wasn't willpower that kept her from indulging in that particular temptation, though. It was shyness, pure and simple.

But it was Halloween—time for make-believe. And tonight, she was going to pretend she was the kind of woman who had the nerve to hit on a sailor, to throw caution to the wind and do wildly sexy things without caring about tomorrow.

As if hearing her thoughts, Livi's companion nudged her arm.

"Look, it's like a roomful of kids trick-or-treating," Tessa drawled. Livi glanced at her best friend as the brunette looked around the bar, humming warmly. The sound was at odds with her halo and fluffy white wings.

Livi laughed. "Sure, if you replace candy with tasty men, and swap kids with horny women out for fun, of course."

"Mmm, no. Not my flavor," Tessa said dismissively, despite her sexy wink at the guy staring at her. Tessa flirted like some women breathed, but she had no interest in military men. "I don't mind indulging your sweet tooth for a while. I'm sure I'll find something to my liking later."

Later, meaning after she'd humored Livi's foray into window-shopping through fantasyland. And Livi knew Tessa wouldn't pressure or berate her for dragging her to a sailor bar where Livi would only sit around mooning over hotties like a high school wallflower before going home alone. Or worse, feeling guilty enough to go with Tessa to her club of choice to watch her flick men off like flies until she found one that interested her.

The petite powerhouse always managed to boil everything down to her favorite common denominator...sex. She did it with a wickedly confident smile and an air of assurance that was probably just as enticing as her curvy body and sultry looks.

Tessa was exactly the kind of woman Livi wished she could be. Oh, they were alike in some ways. Both were fit, smart and savvy. They had tons in common—like Tessa, Livi spoke her mind. She didn't hesitate to talk about the sexy side of life with its myriad pleasures and delights. But unlike her friend, none of that came naturally to her. Hey, neither did one-armed planks, and she'd trained herself to do those.

Livi always thought she'd done a decent job training

herself to ignore her shyness, too. She didn't let her discomfort keep her from doing her job—and given the job she had, that was saying a lot.

Dubbed The Body Babe at twenty, she'd built her initial reputation as a fitness instructor and personal trainer. Certified by ACE, ACSM and AFAA, Livi had a degree in exercise science with a minor in nutrition and had started with dreams of training athletes. That she'd ended up as one of the biggest names in the world of personal training, the founder of Stripped Down Fitness and the star of the Fit To Be Naked videos and training programs wasn't because of her body, and had nothing to do with ambition. She owed all that to her ex-manager absconding with investor funds, leaving her financially screwed. That he was also her ex-husband had been the icing on the cake.

Instead of breaking, as she'd known he'd figured she would, Livi had pulled up her spandex, tightened the laces on her sneakers and rebuilt her career. She'd had a lot of help—yes, including that of strippers. She'd ended up with the Fit To Be Naked program and a reputation as the woman with an ass that bounced quarters and a wicked way with a stripper pole, and she'd made it work.

So it wasn't that she had an issue with sex. Livi loved sex. Once she got to know someone, she was totally comfortable with the subject. And if she hadn't been, the last year spent training, taping and touring with burlesque strippers would have cured that.

More than curing it, Livi had come to realize how much she wanted what they had. Exotic, erotic, pleasure-filled experiences. Relationships, one-nighters, hot times. She no longer had any illusions about love or happy-ever-after. But dammit, she wanted hot sex.

She wanted to find a gorgeous guy, haul him into a quiet corner and see just how hard the Navy made those bodies.

Which was why she was here, she reminded herself.

Since trying to pretend her shyness wasn't an issue hadn't been getting her anywhere, she'd decided to try a different tactic. To simply get the hell over it.

Because she wasn't going to have a great sex life until she did.

So she'd approached her shyness the same way she'd have handled the weight loss of a recalcitrant client. She researched her options, made a list, worked out a schedule and incrementally pushed herself a little more day by day.

Which brought her to tonight.

A fun evening of socializing and maybe a little flirting, with the built-in reward of meeting hot guys who could inspire her fantasies until she was ready for *actual* sex again. And nobody, but nobody, inspired fantasies like sailors did.

And where better to indulge than in the safety of her aunt's bar?

Anticipation zinging through her system, eyes eager for their treats, she scanned the bar, which was filled shoulder-to-shoulder with costumed partiers. After a few seconds and another scan, Livi frowned.

"Where are the Navy hunks?" she wondered, shifting to her tiptoes to see if they were on the other side of the room. At an inch under six feet, she usually didn't have to even stretch her neck to see over most people. But apparently vertical was the theme of this year's Halloween costumes. And while there were a few guys who were obviously sailors, they weren't the yummy kind.

"This bites," she said. "I was so excited for tonight, and now I feel like I got an apple in my trick-or-treat bag."

"And you were looking for a banana?"

Livi laughed then nudged her friend. "C'mon. Maybe we'll find something better on the other side of the bar."

"After pushing through the mob to get this far? No way. Why don't you wave or something to get your aunt's attention. She'll know where the treats are. Maybe she can ring that ship's bell of hers and call them in."

The bell? But everyone would stare at them.

The very thought made her skin crawl. But that's why she was here, Livi reminded herself. Just another opportunity to overcome the debilitating chokehold shyness had on her.

She closed her eyes, took a deep breath and reminded herself she made her living by being stared at. This was no different. It only took her a couple of deep breaths to believe it.

Then with a few murmured apologies, Livi angled herself from her left side to her right through the crowd, pushing her way to the front of the bar. Not an easy task for a woman dressed like a Twinkie. But after a second she caught sight of her aunt's distinctive blue Mohawk.

The older woman jerked her thumb toward a drunk, obviously telling him to get the hell out. The guy was twice her size, but none of her bartenders provided backup. They didn't need to. Nobody messed with Roz. Livi wished that kind of thing were genetic. But search as she might, Livi couldn't find a grain of that sort of confidence in her DNA code.

It wasn't just Roz's looks, although her hair added a good six inches to the slender woman's already impressive height. Nor was it the array of tattoos snaking down her body. Nope, it was authority. Roz exuded it like Tessa exuded sex appeal.

Livi wondered what she exuded. Yawns, most likely.

"Livi!"

She winced when everyone within earshot—and given that Roz was pretty loud, that was a lot of people—turned to stare. Livi pasted on her public smile, ignored the buzzing in her ears and offered her aunt a finger-wiggling wave.

She turned to ask Tessa what she wanted to drink before Roz got there, but her friend was plastered up against a guy wearing a toreador costume, listening as he whispered something in her ear. From the wicked grin on her face, the something was pretty naughty.

"Livi, I didn't think you'd make it," Roz said as she skirted around the bar to give her niece a hug. Not an easy feat given how wide Livi's costume was. Roz stepped back to give her a frowning once-over. "A body like yours, what the hell are you doing dressed like that?"

"Halloween is about the fantasy," Livi explained. "My fantasy is junk food. Since I can't eat it, I figured I'd dress like a Twinkie and be it."

And then there was the cream filling. Her hard, rocking body hadn't inspired any guys to push past her inhibitions and see what she had going on inside. But maybe tonight the subliminal message of her costume would.

"Hey, Roz," Tessa called over Livi's shoulder.

After a few minutes of small talk, her aunt said she had to get back to work. Livi looked around for a comfy barstool to perch on, but Roz had other ideas.

"Now, you girls head to the back room," Roz said, giving Livi a hug as she issued the order. "You can crash the private party there—tell them I sent you. It's quieter, less crowded."

"But I came to see you," Livi protested through a mouth that had gone dry at the words *crash* and *private party.*

"You came to drool over the frogs," Roz said dismissively, referring to the Navy combat divers who frequented her bar. "And you will see me. Later. My relief bartender gets here in twenty minutes, we'll visit then."

Livi wrinkled her nose. Roz always had her pegged, which surprised them both, given that Livi had never met— or even known of—her aunt until two years ago.

"In the meantime…" Roz reached behind them. "I need your help with a party in the back room."

Oh, no. Helping with a party meant facing tons of people. Strange people. Ones she'd never met before.

"Here. Take this with you," she said, handing Livi a foil-covered tray, then giving a second one to Tessa. "You can pretend you're a waitress if it helps."

Livi reluctantly took the tray and the dismissal, even as her mind raced with excuses to get out of going.

"I could really use the help," Roz added. "I'm short-staffed and it's crazy in here."

"I'm not crashing a party. I'll just deliver the food then meet you back here." Knowing the only thing Tessa disliked more than military guys was serving food, Livi gestured toward the tray in her friend's hand. "I can take yours, too, if you want to stay here and enjoy the view."

"You'll change your mind once you see the party," Roz predicted.

"Yummy?" Tessa asked.

"Delicious," Roz confirmed.

"I'm there," Tessa purred, proving once again she didn't have to be interested in partaking to appreciate the view. "C'mon, Livi. Tastiness awaits."

This was why she was here, wasn't it? And playing waitress was the perfect out if it was overwhelming. With that little pep talk and a deep breath, Livi maneuvered her spongy goodness toward the back and prepared to be social.

"Stay close," Livi instructed as she wrapped her free hand around Tessa's so they didn't get separated as they pushed through the crowd.

They barely made it halfway across the room when she felt Tessa slow down. Livi glanced over to see her friend had gone into full-on flirt mode. Hair was being tossed. Her eyes were glittering and her smile had taken on a wicked glint.

"Target spotted," Tessa said, making as if to break away.

"Oh, no, you don't," Livi said, laughing as she tugged

Tessa along. She used her Twinkie bulk to push through the bodies, pulling her friend in her wake. "You're crashing this party with me, remember? I'm sure there are plenty of men in there for you to choose from."

"Yeah, okay. He had a small dick, anyway," Tessa said as they reached the hall leading to the private section of the bar.

Her hand on the doorknob, Livi threw a frown toward Tessa's rejected target. "How could you tell that?"

"The way he was sitting." Tessa tilted her head so her hair flowed in a dark wave over one bare shoulder before shimmying a little so the fabric fell across her breasts just so. Then she offered Livi a wink. "He had his legs crossed above the knee, did you notice? No guy with a dick big enough to satisfy me can cross higher than the ankle."

For a brief second, Livi could only goggle. Then she laughed so hard her nerves dissipated. And that, she realized, was probably why Tessa had said what she had.

Then again, Tessa knew a lot about dicks. So maybe she was being supportive *and* telling the truth.

"You know, if you were actually as oversexed as you pretend to be, you'd have dropped dead from exhaustion years ago," Livi said, still giggling as she pushed open the door.

They made it two steps inside before stopping.

"Oh, boy," Tessa murmured. "Now there's a treat I wouldn't mind showing a trick or two."

Livi mentally echoed that with a purr.

Oh, boy, indeed.

The room was filled with men, all so gorgeous they blurred into a yummy candy store in Livi's mind. It was a good night when a woman could choose between a gladiator, a kilted highlander and a bare-chested fireman.

But Livi only had eyes for the superhero.

Deep in conversation with another guy, he might have

been sitting in the corner, but he still seemed to be in command of the entire room. He had a power vibe.

And he was a super hottie.

His hair was as black as midnight, and it brought to mind all sorts of fun things to do at that hour. The supershort cut accentuated the shape of his face with its sharp cheekbones and strong jawline. His eyes were light, but she couldn't tell the color from where she was standing. Livi wet her suddenly dry lips and forced her gaze lower, wondering if the rest of him lived up to the promise of that gorgeous face.

Her heart did a slow thumpity-thump as her eyes meandered over his broad shoulders and down muscular arms encased in a tight blue shirt. She sighed her appreciation at the definition of his pecs beneath the bright letter *S* on his chest.

The man of steel. She wondered if he was hard *all* over.

Then he grinned at something his companion said.

And Livi got shaky. Her knees melted, her thighs trembled and nipples sprang to attention. That was an orgasm smile. She'd heard the girls at the club talk about those during training sessions, but she'd figured strippers exaggerated everything from their bumps to their grinds.

But now she knew.

All he'd have to add to that smile was an offer and she'd climax for sure. And she'd bet that alone would be better than the two years of sex she'd had with her ex.

"C'mon," Tessa said, her tone as impatient as if Livi had made her wait an hour instead of a few lust-filled seconds. Whether it was because she knew her prodding wasn't enough to get Livi's feet moving or because she just loved the attention, Tessa raised her voice, along with her tray, and called out, "Who's hungry?"

All eyes turned their way.

Tessa preened.

Livi felt like a deer caught in the headlights. Her bubble

of lust burst under a dozen or so pairs of eyes and panic took its place. Deep breath, she told herself. And another. By the third her nerves were under control and her public persona firmly in place.

"Roz asked us to bring food," she said in the same cheery tone she used to tell women to grab a pole and straddle it like a stallion. She tilted her tray to prove they weren't *really* crashing the party.

"Food and guests—we'll take them both."

"C'mon in and join us."

"The party just got interesting."

Tessa took the warm chorus of welcomes at face value, sashaying across the room to begin introducing herself like the social butterfly she was.

Livi was more like a caterpillar than a butterfly, though.

Nerves danced in her stomach, keeping time with the buzzing in her ears. But Livi forced herself to cross the room. Chin high, smile sassy, she knew nobody looking at her could see her anxiety. She'd had years of practice at looking way more confident than she'd ever feel.

She didn't let herself look toward the corner where Super Hottie was sitting, in case he returned her interest. He probably hadn't even noticed their arrival. But still… It was difficult enough to sashay into a room full of strangers. She didn't need to be self-conscious, too.

"Roz didn't have to go to any trouble," said a sweet-faced brunette dressed as a sleek black cat as she hurried forward to meet Livi. "She already provided enough food to feed, well, the Navy."

The woman gestured to the crowd in case Livi didn't realize the male half of the room were sailors out of uniform.

But Livi didn't have to be told.

One, the bar, Olive Oyl's, was in Coronado and catered to the naval base. Two, Roz didn't close off half her bar for anyone but sailors. And three, well, just look at the guys. They were the epitome of all things military, from their fit bodies to their buzz haircuts to their powerful demeanor— even the guy dressed like a duck.

"Roz figured it'd been a while since dinner and thought people might be hungry. She has a need to feed," Livi said with a smile and a shrug. "She brought cupcakes and lasagna to my catered wedding, just in case, and I quote, 'the caterer sucked and the cake was boring-ass vanilla.'"

She bit her lip. Should she have said 'ass'? Maybe she should have just kept quiet. She never knew if her words would be taken right or not.

But the other woman's appreciative laugh eased her discomfort. Livi set the tray on the table and uncovered it, then stepped back as a dozen people attacked the egg rolls and nachos.

"Looks as if Roz knew what she was talking about," the woman remarked, her expression slightly stunned.

"She always does." Roz had even told Livi not to bother changing her last name, since the marriage wouldn't last long enough for the paperwork to get filed.

"I'm Eden," the cat said, holding out her hand. "You must be Roz's niece."

Livi blinked, wondering how she'd guessed. Most people didn't believe them when they were straight-out told, since the only shared trait—physical or personality-wise— between Roz and Livi was their height. Few people knew them both well enough to realize how alike they were, from their taste for green tea to their love of animals.

Aha.

"Eden the vet?" Livi asked. "Purveyor of furry addictions and cuddly friends?"

"Oh, you met Pedro?" Eden exclaimed.

At ease now, Livi fell into a delighted discussion about her aunt's new three-legged cat.

But her nerves still fluttered, like the wings of a nagging butterfly. Not about the crowd. She'd found someone to talk to. Nope, these were sexual nerves. The kind that were inspired by curiosity and fed by desire. The kind she hadn't felt in, oh, about a million years.

Unable to resist any longer, sure they'd settle once she assured herself he wasn't paying any attention to her, Livi looked toward the corner.

The lair of Super Hottie, the sexiest man in the room.

She blinked.

Livi's butterflies turned into fighter jets, roaring through her system. She locked her knees against the trembling and thanked God that the thick foam of her costume hid her instantly rock-hard nipples.

Because he was staring.

At her.

And he looked as if he liked what he saw.

Uh-oh.

WELL, WELL. Lt. Commander Mitch Donovan leaned against the wall and watched the gorgeous blonde dressed as a Twinkie talk to Sullivan's wife. Mitch had never had much of a sweet tooth. But right now he had an intense desire for a taste.

A mellow grin played over his mouth as his gaze drifted down the length of her golden sponge cake–shaped body. How could a woman covered in that inspire lust at first sight? Then his eyes wandered lower, to where the costume ended at mid-thigh. Those were some damned sexy legs, from what he could see. His eyes lifted to her face again and his lust kicked up a notch.

As a man who was used to excelling in extremes of all kinds, he appreciated his body's instant reaction. He just didn't quite understand the Pavlovian intensity of it.

She was pretty. Her honey-blond hair was twisted back,

leaving her face bare. Dark brows contrasted with the color of her hair and slashed over eyes that seemed to be taking in the entire room at once.

His gaze narrowed. Her expression was friendly, her body language relaxed. But the hand she'd tucked into the side of her costume clenched and unclenched, her fingers fluttering over the foam.

Intrigued by the contrast—always curious when confronted with even the hint of a puzzle—he glanced back at her face to search for other signs. Of fear. Of nerves. Of…

Mitch's brain went blank.

He didn't think it'd ever done that before in his life. But it was blank, so he couldn't be sure.

All he could see were those eyes. Huge, filled with so many emotions he didn't understand. Lashes so lush they cast a shadow around those eyes, giving her the look of a startled doe. A very sexy, very appealing startled doe.

"Irish."

Who was she? He held her gaze, imagining those big eyes staring up at him as he poised over her body. Wondering if she'd keep them open after he'd plunged inside or if she'd close them and ride out the ecstasy.

"Yo, you want a drink?"

She blinked, those thick lashes brushing the delicate curve of her cheeks. The move should have broken the spell, but Mitch still couldn't look away. She wet her lips, the pink tip of her tongue briefly sliding over the full cushion of her bottom lip. He was glad he'd opted for jeans with his costume instead of tights. The zipper didn't offer much give against his sudden erection, but he was hard enough that he'd have ripped right through a pair of tights, superhero-issue or not.

What did she taste like? Hot and mysterious? Sweet and tempting? How long would it take before he could find out?

"Mitch. Donovan. Lt. Commander, dammit."

Mitch blinked.

Frowned.

What?

He turned his head, meeting Chief Petty Officer Gabriel Thorne's impatient stare.

Damn.

"That's Lt. Commander, dammit, sir," Mitch shot back. "And what's your problem?"

"I've been talking, but you're not listening. I've gotta tell you, Irish, I'm not used to being ignored."

Mitch's lips twitched. Truer words were never spoken.

Shirtless, wearing buckskins and a feather behind his ear, Gabriel Thorne—call sign Romeo—was a man who thrived on attention. And he had plenty to thrive on. Mitch had served with the guy for six years off and on, and he'd never once seen him get shot down. Actually, Mitch wasn't sure he'd ever seen Romeo make the first move. The guy was usually too busy fending off the women to need to.

"Since I don't plan to go home with you tonight, I'm not worried about bruising your ego," he told his friend, happy to gloss right over the temporary and mind-boggling fog of lust. Mitch wouldn't let himself look toward the blonde again. Not until he'd had a chance to analyze what had happened and figure out how she'd managed to short-circuit his brain.

"My ego is Teflon," Gabriel assured him, his black eyes dancing with amusement aimed at the both of them. Native American blood ran strong in Thorne, from the hint of blue in his close-cut hair to the gold of his skin and razor-sharp cheekbones. "Besides, it's not just the ladies who pay close attention, my friend. I knock, the enemy listens."

"Might have a little to do with the IED you're aiming their way," Mitch pointed out with a grin. A demolitions expert, Thorne could make a grenade dance around a corner, scurry down a hall or chase a man up a mountain.

"But don't let me rain all over your fantasy with my bor-ing reality."

"Bro, my reality is most guys' fantasy." Gabriel winked. "But then, so is yours. Navy SEAL, fast-tracking your way through the ranks with enough medals and commendations to cover a wall. And you're not bad-looking, so you don't scare away the ladies when they're hitting on me. All in all, I'd say we're a damned good team."

"Yep," Mitch agreed, draining his beer. Gabriel liked to say he kept Mitch around as a wingman because most guys couldn't handle his success with the ladies.

Mitch knew better, but it didn't bother him enough to correct his friend.

"So you wanna fill me in?"

"Not really." Mitch didn't have to ask what Gabriel meant. He'd known his little trip into the lusty fog wouldn't go unnoticed.

"She came in with the brunette with the broken halo. They're not connected with any of the team, so I figure Roz sent them. Either that or they're enemy infiltrators, here to deliver food and steal our Halloween secrets."

Impressed, Mitch grinned and shook his head. It was hard to be irritated with the guy's uncanny insights when they were always delivered with a laugh.

"What? You don't have her name? A detailed dossier on her likes and dislikes, contact information and bra size?"

"Hey, I'm in explosives, not intelligence."

"Ahh," Mitch said, drawing the word out.

In true Romeo fashion, the other man arched one brow and nodded. Challenge accepted.

"Five," Gabriel said, referring to the number of minutes he guaranteed it'd take him to win the challenge.

"Bet," Mitch confirmed, agreeing to their usual terms.

Five minutes was enough time to make sure he had con-trol over his reactions—both north and south of his belt.

Gabriel stood, grabbed their empty beer bottles and sauntered across the room. He didn't head for the blonde, though. Instead he lost himself in the crowd around the pool table.

Less than a minute later he was back with four beers, a slight frown and the brunette with the broken halo and a body made to tempt Satan.

"Mitch, this is Tessa. She was nice enough to bring our food since my hands are full."

Mitch arched a brow. He'd had to resort to a lame excuse like that to get the woman over? Romeo was losing his touch.

Ignoring Mitch's grin, Gabriel took the plate of egg rolls.

"These are great. But you're too gorgeous to be with catering," Gabriel said, leaning back on his heels and giving the angel an assessing look. "How'd you get roped into playing waitress?"

The brunette matched him look for look, then shrugged.

"Roz asked, so Livi and I delivered."

Mitch glanced at his watch.

"Livi? Isn't that Roz's niece?"

Mitch almost rolled his eyes. Damned if the man didn't belong in intelligence. Of course, the only way he'd be any good there was if the US needed to infiltrate a harem guarded by women on an all-female island. But that was beside the point.

"You're wanting to meet Livi?" the brunette said slowly, giving Gabriel a long look before turning those assessing eyes on Mitch. He was pretty sure those baby blues garnered as much info on him in that single look as the Pentagon had in their last security check. The military had approved his clearance. He wasn't so sure the angel would.

No big deal. It wasn't like he needed a wingman—or in this case wingman and winged woman—to get the girl.

Before Mitch could brush off the sultry angel, she turned and gave a low whistle, waving her friend over.

While she did, Gabriel lifted his wrist to show he was on minute three of five.

But Mitch wasn't paying attention.

His focus was the Twinkie, who after a moment's hesitation crossed the room to join them.

Mitch knew there were words being said.

He was sure he was missing out on the fun of watching Romeo strike out.

But the closer the blonde came, the deeper into that fog of lust Mitch fell.

Brown. Her eyes were the color of melted milk chocolate. Rich, warm and inviting. Up close her face was even more striking in its delicacy. Especially the contrast of those dark eyes and brows against her pale skin and golden hair.

Those rich, hypnotic eyes met his.

Mitch could see interest there. And heat. Oh, yeah. A smile played at the corner of his mouth. He recognized that heat.

He opened his mouth to introduce himself. Before he could, Romeo snapped his fingers.

"Olivia Kane."

The blonde blinked, frowned and pulled her gaze away from Mitch to look at Gabriel.

"Yes?"

Mitch grimaced. He didn't have to look at his watch to know it had been just under five minutes.

"I'm a big fan. I'd love to talk about your training programs. Excuse me just one second, though." Gabriel glanced at Mitch and grinned. "Thirty-six bravo, and out."

2

"I'M MITCH DONOVAN. And you're Olivia?"

Unable to find words, Livi simply nodded and nestled her hand into Mitch's much warmer, much *larger* one.

It was like grabbing a live wire. His touch zapped a shaft of hot desire through her system with so much intensity, Livi wanted to lie down. On the nearest flat surface, preferably with him on top of her.

She could run a four-minute mile, lead an advanced interval-training class for fifty women while giving detailed verbal instructions, or handle herself in the kickboxing ring against a toothless bruiser named Bubba.

And she could do them all with a big smile, an average maximum heart rate of 120, and absolute faith her training meant that even if she got distracted by talking, muscle memory would get her through the workout.

But right now her smile was as shaky as her knees. Her heart was beating so fast and loud that she was lightheaded, and her muscles were going into meltdown.

All it had taken was a single touch from Super Hottie.

Or…

Um, what had he said his name was?

Livi wet her lips, about to ask, when she realized she was still shaking his hand. No, it'd been so long now that she was just *holding* his hand.

Could she be a bigger dork?

Her cheeks warming, she let go and stepped back. It took all of her resolve, and the image of her mother's glare, to keep Livi from turning heel and running out of the room.

And she'd thought she'd overcome her shyness? Ha. Making a complete ass of herself with the sexiest man she'd met in forever pretty much burst that illusion.

Then she forced herself to stop. This was simply resistance. Maybe a dash of humiliation, but mostly resistance. Muscles weren't built without it, she reminded herself. *See it as a strength-training exercise.*

Rallying to the self-lecture, Livi took a slow, subtle breath, pulling the air all the way down to her belly button. She let it calm her, soothe the edgy nerves. Another breath and she was able to pull on her meet-the-press persona, complete with toothy smile.

"Most people call me Livi," she told him before inclining her head toward his friend, who appeared to be arguing with Tessa.

But... Men never argued with Tessa.

"I'm surprised he recognized me in this getup," Livi said slowly, distracted by the other two. "Actually, I'm surprised he recognized me at all. That doesn't happen very often."

"Romeo has a special knack," Super Hottie said with a friendly shrug. "I keep telling him he'd be a great spy, but his memory is pretty selective."

"Romeo?" Tessa stopped whatever she was debating so fiercely to interrupt. She gave Super Hottie's half-dressed friend an amused look then flicked her finger over the feather behind his ear. "And here I thought you were Tonto."

"And here I thought angels were sweet," the man called Romeo shot back.

Livi's confused glance bounced between the two of them. Tessa seduced men. She didn't argue with them. And the only guy Livi had ever seen go toe to toe with her usually charming friend had done so because he'd wanted to wear the feather boa in a dance number.

What was going on?

Frowning, she looked at Super Hottie askance. He gave a baffled shake of his head.

"So what do you do if you're not a spy?" Livi asked Romeo, with a bright smile, trying to smooth over the social awkwardness. An odd change since she was usually the one causing it.

"I blow things up." His smile coated in charm, he leaned back, draping one arm over the back of the chair. "Irish here does push-ups."

Oh, the images.

Livi's heart did a happy bounce just thinking of Super Hottie in a plank position, biceps and triceps bulging as he pressed. Up. Down. Up. Down.

Whew. She wet her lips and wished she had a glass of water. Iced, preferably.

As much to try to erase the tempting visual from her mind as to stop the conversation before it moved on, Livi waved her hand in the air.

"Hold up. Romeo? Irish? I have trouble believing your mother looked at your sweet baby faces and decided to give you those names."

Romeo gave a snort that could have been taken as amusement if not for the quick flash of bitterness in his eyes.

Super Hottie flew to the rescue so fast Livi wondered if she had been imagining things.

"Romeo and Irish are call signs, nicknames, if you will. It's a Navy thing, or rather a military thing." Super Hottie offered a smile that rivaled his friend's in charm. "I'd rather you just called me Mitch, though. And he's Gabriel, if you were looking for something else to call him."

"I've got a few other things in mind," Tessa muttered.

Mitch. Livi was too busy rolling Super Hottie's name around in her mind to do more than give her friend a quick elbow jab.

"So Gabriel blows things up," Livi said, her eyes locked

on Mitch's bright blue ones. They were hypnotic. Seductively hypnotic. "What about you, Mitch? What do you do?"

Me, she wanted to suggest. *I'd like you to do me.*

But for once, her bone-deep shyness came to the rescue, keeping her mouth shut before she blurted that out.

"I'm a bit of master of everything. You name it, I've probably done it."

"Is that so?" Livi murmured, her mind rapidly compiling a list of things he might have mastered. Since most of them involved him being naked, her smile turned naughty. "Tell me more."

"Why don't you name a few and we'll compare notes." Coming from any other guy, she'd consider that to be a pickup line. But Mitch looked as sincere as he did amused. He was so nonthreatening, he scared her.

Or maybe that was the desire pounding through her body.

She wet her lips, wondering how to find out.

Before she could come up with any ideas, Tessa's words caught her attention.

"Livi can beat that. She is the push-up queen."

Frowning, Livi looked at her best friend. Had she missed the coronation?

"I bow to her majesty's prowess. But Irish is still the best."

Was he? He was busy watching the debate between Gabriel and Tessa, so Livi allowed herself to stare. He definitely had a great body. She could see enough of his muscle definition to give a nod to the Navy for a job well done. A great body was one thing. Knowing how to use it was another.

Been there, done that, had the divorce papers to prove it.

She was pretty sure Mitch knew what to do with his. A guy as hot as he was, as focused and intuitive? He had to, right?

"You want to bet?"

"Name the stakes, Angel."

"Anything you want says that Livi can beat Mitch at push-ups."

Livi blinked as the words filtered through her fantasies of what Mitch might do if he focused on her naked body.

What?

She shook her head then did a mental replay.

"What?" She gave Tessa a baffled look. "What are you talking about?"

"Just pointing out that you're in great shape and you rock at push-ups." Tessa shrugged. "Why not prove it?"

"Maybe because I'm dressed like a snack cake." Then Livi muttered out the side of her mouth. "Or maybe because I don't want to? Besides, you're in great shape, too. *You* prove it."

"You've got a bodysuit on underneath." Ignoring the rest, Tessa frowned. Obviously she was more focused on beating Romeo at whatever private game they were playing than on Livi's wants.

"You're seriously challenging my guy to a push-up contest?" His teeth flashed white against his bronze skin before Gabriel threw back his head and laughed. "Angel, he's a SEAL. Best of the best. I know your girl is good, but she can't be that good."

A SEAL?

Livi melted a little inside.

He really was Super Hottie.

Livi's eyes flew back to Mitch. He'd angled his chair so it was tilted against the wall, his booted foot on his knee. He watched Gabriel and Tessa continue their heated debate, his smile not shifting. Then he met Livi's gaze and shrugged as if to say he knew their friends were acting crazy, but what could he do.

For the first time in her life, Livi considered ditching her friend and asking a guy to take her home.

Then she could show him what she could do. Or better yet, he could show her.

"C'mon, Liv. I'll help you out of your costume."

"What?" Livi shook her head, wondering if that halo was squeezing Tessa's head too tight. "I'm not taking off my clothes."

The words had barely left her mouth when she felt it.

The air changed.

Electrified.

Startled, she looked back at Mitch.

His calm amusement was gone. Instead, his eyes were intense. Filled with an unmistakable sexual energy that sparked a response so hot and fast Livi swore she had a tiny orgasm then and there.

"How about a private bet?" he suggested quietly, his smile making it clear he was once again amused by the entire scenario.

Livi frowned. Was he always so mellow and self-assured? The confidence might be a SEAL thing. His friend had it, too. But where Gabriel came across somewhere between confident and cocky, Mitch was simply sure.

What was that like?

Had the man never lost at anything?

Livi had no idea where the urge came from. She was clueless how the words landed on the tip of her tongue. But before she could stop it, her own challenge tumbled out.

"You're on," she agreed, leaning forward until she was nose to nose with him. For a second she lost her train of thought as his scent, rich and spicy, wrapped around her. His eyes were pure blue, she realized. Not a hint of gray or green. Gorgeous.

And amused.

It was the amusement that snapped her back.

"I'll double whatever they bet," she said, tilting her head to indicate Tessa and Gabriel.

"I'm going to enjoy this," Mitch promised quietly.

Livi hoped she did, too.

Five minutes later, the parameters had been set, enough spectators had realized a challenge was afoot and a crowd was gathering.

Was she crazy?

"So you really think you can beat him?" Tessa murmured as she unzipped the foam under Livi's arm.

Hell, no.

"Why are we doing this?" she sidestepped. "Can't we just have drinks with the guys and flirt?"

"Flirt?" Tessa's face curled into a combination of horror, disdain and something else. Something Livi couldn't read. "You're kidding, right? We're not flirting with these guys. We're beating them then taking our winnings and getting out of here."

"I'd rather flirt."

Which was saying a lot, since flirting tended to make her feel like she'd just broken out in a rash.

"The guy is a SEAL." Tessa said that the same way she'd state that he was a puppy-kicking Peeping Tom with a chicken fetish.

"So?"

"So, Pauline would have a cow if she found out. You know how she feels about Navy guys. She'd have a total meltdown, bitch for months and probably book you on a gig in Timbuktu to get you away from him."

Livi wrinkled her nose but couldn't disagree.

Pauline was Livi's manager, the driving force behind Livi's success. She'd managed, maneuvered and manipulated Livi into an enviable career, where she was currently teetering on the edge of fame and fortune.

Livi didn't figure any of that gave the woman the right to call the shots on her personal life.

Pauline was Livi's mother. The last time Livi had ignored her demands disguised as advice, she'd married Derrick. The price of her mother stepping in to clean up that mess had been a blanket promise to not do anything stupid again.

Livi inspected Mitch.

He was hot. He was sexy. He was seriously appealing.

And he had enough charisma to shut down her brain.

Did that qualify as stupid?

Livi felt like Eve standing in an apple orchard. And the hottie with the big *S* on his chest was the biggest, juiciest, tastiest apple of the bunch. Did she follow the rules?

Or did she give in to temptation?

Duh. Like there was a choice.

"We'll just make sure Pauline doesn't find out," she murmured.

"No," Tessa protested. "Have pity. I'm a part of your crew. If you're shipped off to Timbuktu, I'm stuck there with you."

Livi pulled her gaze away from Mitch to give Tessa an arch look.

"Double dates with Dean Wickens, that drummer guy, Paul who never would admit his last name and those creepy twins," she recited, ticking each off on her fingers. "Endless clubs, three production parties and my favorite pair of sneakers covered in purple paint."

Tessa's face froze. Her eyes shifted to the corner then she lifted her chin. "What's all that have to do with Timbuktu?"

"In every one of those situations, you promised you'd owe me." Livi inclined her head toward the corner. "I'm calling in your debt."

"Dammit." Tessa huffed and crossed her arms over her chest to glare. When Livi's expression didn't change, Tessa rolled her eyes and threw her hands in the air. "Fine. I won't tell Pauline."

Livi rounded her brow. Tessa pressed her lips tight and gave a sigh strong enough to knock over a horse.

"God, you're demanding. Okay, yes, I'll stay with you and play backup." Tessa huffed. "But only for an hour. No double dates."

"Works for me," Livi agreed, almost giddy with excitement. "But just so I know, what's your problem with Gabriel? I know you don't go for military guys, but I've never seen you get straight-up ugly with one before."

"He's just so unbelievably arrogant, like he's so sure he's perfect and knows everyone is just waiting to appreciate him." The glare she shot across the room made it clear that disagreeing was pointless, so Livi hummed instead. "He's obviously got a one-track mind. He thinks sex is the be-all and end-all. And who the hell looks that perfect?"

Scanning from the top of Tessa's perfectly tousled curls down her perfectly curved body to her perfectly polished toes, Livi could only shake her head.

"The mind boggles," was all she could say without bursting into laughter.

From her narrow-eyed look, Tessa caught the amusement, anyway. She was silent for a moment then shook her head and changed the subject.

"So, bottom line, can you win?" she asked. "Can you take Mitch?"

"Yeah," Livi promised. "I'm taking him."

With that, she stepped away. She pulled her arms free and shifted her head through the unzipped foam.

Her eyes locked on Mitch's as she stepped out of the costume, her body clad in a pale yellow racer-backed unitard. Maybe Livi had a touch of social anxiety, and she might not have anywhere near Mitch's confidence. She might have a few insecurities and a whole slew of worries. Throw in a domineering mother, an absentee father, a soul-sucking ex-husband and a ticking time clock on her career, and she had a lot of baggage.

But what she also had—and she was positive of this—was a rockin' awesome body. She worked on it every day. She made her living with it.

And she was going to use it to win this bet.

HOLY HELL, SHE was a Playboy centerfold wrapped in a wet dream mixed with an erotic version of the girl next door.

Sexy and sweet, gorgeous and…

Mitch's brain shut off again as every particle of his being focused on Livi's body. She was perfect. Like her face, her body was a contrast of strong and delicate. Broad shoulders and lightly muscled arms framed full breasts and a delicately tapered waist. Her slender hips curved out nonetheless. And those legs…

Mitch gave a silent groan as his gaze meandered down legs so perfectly shaped, so temptingly long, that it'd take him hours to appreciate them the way they deserved.

"You wanna wipe the drool off your chin?"

"What?" Mitch realized what he was doing. He gave his friend a hard look. "What the hell is going on?"

Gabriel pulled a contemplative face, leaned back in his chair and locked his hands behind head.

"Hmm, if I had to guess, I'd say you're horny for the Twinkie. And seeing as how her body has made many a man sit up and beg, that's not a surprise."

How many a man? And how *had* Romeo recognized Livi?

"Details," Mitch demanded.

"She's the hottest thing to hit fitness in years," Gabriel told him. He grinned at Mitch's haughty look. "I dated a gal who was trying to get on her workout team. Olivia Kane,

The Body Babe. I watched a few of her videos with Casey. Or was it Carey?"

"You should keep records," Mitch suggested, shaking his head. "Or maybe figure out a mnemonic rhyme to remember who's who."

"Not enough letters in the alphabet for that, Bro."

But Mitch wasn't paying attention anymore. He was busy watching Livi stretch one arm over her head and catch her fingers with the other behind her back. The move pushed her shoulder blades together and lifted her breasts higher. His body went into overdrive, lust pounding through him in throbbing waves.

Mitch wasn't a horn dog. Not like Romeo pretended to be. He appreciated women, and had definitely had more than his share. And like Romeo, he never had to pursue them. Which made it easy to walk away. When he was redeployed. When he was sent on a mission. When he was ready to move on. Mitch only had one true passion, one focus.

His career.

Livi bent in half, her hands flat on the floor, butt high and back arched, so she faced forward. Her ponytail swung in time with the pulsing moves she made to warm up and stretch out her muscles.

For the first time in his life, he wondered if he had room for another passion.

"You looking to start something up with her?" Romeo asked, his tone low and quiet. "If you do, be careful."

Mitch tore his gaze off the sloping muscles of Livi's back and shoulders to the man next to him.

"Careful? Her friend might have 'man-eater' written all over her, but Livi doesn't strike me as the kind of woman who needs a warning label."

"Take it from me, she's even more dangerous. She's the relationship kind." Romeo gave a sage nod. Then he eyed Mitch and added, "Course, just because I'm relationship poison doesn't mean you are. I don't want to be a bad influence on you. Maybe you ought to give a relationship a try. You might like it."

And what if he did? There was no way a man could have two priorities. Could he put his career goals in second place?

"Not going to happen," he said, as much to himself as to his friend. "I'm leaving at first light for Virginia Beach to report to DEVGRU screening, remember."

DEVGRU, the Navy's counter-terrorism group, was the elite of the elite. Reporting to Naval Special Warfare Command, the unit often worked with the CIA and always operated in the dark. The invitation to screen was an honor, regardless of whether Mitch made it through training—or even chose to try.

He gave a silent groan as Livi shifted. She was grabbing her ankles now, her face pressed to her knees and her butt temptingly high in the air.

Enticement like this, he'd never seen in his life. This kind of enticement made a man think twice about assignments, regret deployments.

Mitch firmed his jaw—might as well, since everything else had firmed up—and shook his head. That wasn't going to happen to him. His old man had done that. Not that Mitch didn't think his mother was pretty awesome, because he did. But if his grandfather, the Admiral, had pointed it out once, he'd pointed it out a million times. If Thomas Donovan had put his career ahead of his personal life, he'd have been a vice admiral instead of a captain.

Of course, the old man always responded by reminding his father that if he'd been as career-obsessed as he, he wouldn't have his son. So Mitch couldn't fault the decision too much.

But that didn't mean he was going to follow it.

"You know, Irish, she's damned good. She might actually take you." Romeo grinned at the crowd gathering around. Tessa waved her hand high in the air, calling for the attention of anyone who hadn't already wandered over. "It's going to be painful when she does, too. There's gotta be three teams here to bear witness. Good thing it's not our platoon."

He and Romeo usually deployed on the east coast. They were only in Coronado for the next few months to take part in a new training program. But the SEALs were a small family. What one platoon knew, the others would soon know, too. Nobody ferreted out secrets like SEALs.

Mitch wasn't worried. He didn't lose.

"What's going on here?" a loud voice called out.

Greetings and exclamations flew through the room as Roz Evans appeared, a tray of sandwiches in each hand and bats hanging from her ears. This was her one concession to Halloween, Mitch knew, since the foot-tall blue hair was everyday wear.

"I hear you boys are causing a ruckus," she said a couple minutes later, after she'd handed off the sandwiches.

"Would I do that?" Mitch asked, offering her his most charming smile.

"You might not," she acknowledged before tilting her head at Romeo. "But this one would."

"Only because you keep turning me down."

Livi and Tessa arrived just in time to hear Gabriel's declaration. Tessa's frown was as deep as Livi's smile was bright.

"You know these guys?" Livi asked, handing Roz a beer.

"Darlin', when will you learn? I know everybody."

"You'll play ref for our little contest, won't you?" Tessa asked.

"Sure thing. I got the deets on the contest when I came in." She pointed to the center of the room. She didn't have to say another word before four guys were there moving tables and chairs to clear a wide circle. "Who's covering the bet?"

"That'd be me." Wearing a T-shirt with the face of the Cookie Monster on it, Bad Ass Brody Lane sauntered over with a fistful of cash. "Who're you going with, Roz?"

"Donovan, I know you're a kick-ass SEAL, and usually I'd put all my money on you," she said, pulling a few bills out of her pocket and counting twenty into Bad Ass's waiting hand. "But all things considered, I'm gonna have to back my girl."

"You got this," Brody assured him.

More than ready to find out, Mitch got to his feet.

"Shall we?" he suggested, waving his hand to indicate the *ring.*

Livi took a deep breath that gave a first-rate demonstration of the wonders of Lycra and did a little stretching of Mitch's libido, too. She walked just a step ahead, giving him an up-close and excellent view of her butt.

Mitch had been competing most of his life. Against others, against himself, against the enemy.

He'd never competed against temptation, though.

This was going to be interesting.

3

"ARE YOU SURE about this?" Mitch asked Livi.

She hadn't volunteered for this little competition. More like she'd been railroaded. So he figured it was only fair to give her an out.

"Oh, I'm sure," she said quietly. "How about you?"

Damn, she was cute with that challenging look in her eyes and her chin in the air. He'd take it easy, like he did with the kids he sometimes coached, so she felt good about the results.

"Standard push-ups?" Roz asked, accepting Cade Sullivan's hand and stepping onto a chair for prime referee viewing.

"For the queen," Gabriel decided. "Irish does military-style."

"I'm sure glad I have you making these decisions for me," Mitch told his friend.

"I figure you'd be lost without me." Romeo smacked him on the back then stepped out of the circle. "I'll count for Irish."

"Let's keep it a little more impartial than that," Roz suggested. She scanned the crowd. "Cade, you count for Mitch and Eden can count for Livi."

Commander Cade Sullivan moved in front of Mitch with a wink and a grin. Wearing puppy-dog ears as a nod to Halloween, the guy had a rep as one of the toughest BUD/S instructors to hit SEAL training.

His wife scooped up the tail of her cat costume and took

a similar position on the other side of Roz's chair. At the last minute she rushed forward to give Livi a quick hug.

"No hug for me?" Mitch asked Cade.

"You're not pretty enough," Sullivan dismissed. "Now drop and give me fifty."

"Take your positions," Roz called out, holding up her cell phone. "One minute on the clock."

Livi dropped to the floor and assumed the plank position. Mitch followed suit, angling himself so he could watch her. Keeping an eye on the competition was just smart thinking. Besides, when his gaze shifted to the shadowed valley between her breasts, the view was damned nice.

"And..." Roz gave a shrill whistle. "Go."

Hands shoulder-width apart, elbows tucked against his body, Mitch went. Down, up. Down, up. He didn't count. He just let his body do its job. Instantly in rhythm, he glanced at Livi.

She was staring right at him as she pumped up and down.

"I could do this all night," she murmured. "How about you?"

Mitch grinned.

"Did you know that push-ups are one of the best exercises you can do for your sex life?" she asked, her voice so low that given their position on the floor, he doubted anybody in the cheering crowd had heard her.

But he had.

His body stiffened in reaction. Good thing he was wearing jeans instead of sweatpants. Otherwise his push-ups would have turned into pole vaults.

"It's all about the core," Livi continued, her words spaced with her breathing. "You strengthen those core muscles and yowza. You know I work with strippers, right? The things they tell me a good core can do are pretty amazing."

Shit.

He missed a beat, his elbow locking. He had to do the next push-up one-armed to find his rhythm again.

He'd rappelled off a cliff in a shower of bullets.

He'd shot, sniper-style, dangling from a helicopter while militants targeted it with IEDs.

He'd built his reputation on his ability to focus. To go after what he wanted, ignoring any and all distractions.

"Thirty seconds."

Mitch ripped his gaze from the view of Livi's arms, with their perfectly rounded muscles bunching and stretching. Her strength was almost as much a turn-on as her gorgeous body.

"Mmm, you've got some kind of stamina," she observed in that same quiet tone, her words a little breathier now.

Is that how she'd sound during sex?

Imagining it, Mitch looked over. Her eyes gleamed hot with desire as she stared at his arms. Her lips were pursed as she sucked air in, blew it out.

Then her eyes shifted to meet his.

And she smiled.

A wicked smile that nearly sent him flat on his face.

"Fifty-five seconds."

Damn it.

Jaw clenched, Mitch called up his much-touted focus, staring straight ahead.

Up. Down. Up. Down.

Nothing else entered his mind, nothing else mattered.

Up. Down.

"Time."

More winded than he usually was in a minute, Mitch did a final push, pulling his knees to his chest and vaulting into a crouch. He didn't let himself look at Livi.

Not yet.

Instead, he watched Eden give a shout of delight, quickly followed by a hip-bump to her husband.

"She kicked butt," she claimed.

Cade's smile was indulgent, but he shook his head.

"Sorry, babe. But he kicked butt."

"Flirt on your own time," Roz instructed. "What's the count?"

"Sixty-nine," Eden declared with a triumphant smile.

"Sixty-nine," Cade said at the same time.

A tie? Well, well.

Not sure if he was more impressed with Livi's tactics or amused at the entire scenario, Mitch grinned.

The room exploded in applause.

Romeo and Tessa went toe to toe, debating the results at the top of their lungs.

Her breath labored, Livi rested her forehead on her knee for a second before meeting Mitch's gaze. Her eyes were filled with delight, her smile as much a turn-on as her physical prowess.

She tilted her head toward the arguing couple and arched one brow.

"What are the stakes they're fighting so fiercely over?" Mitch shrugged, surprised to discover his arms were on fire. He was used to pushing his body to the limits, but it was obviously harder when half his blood supply had taken up residence below his belt.

"Yo, Romeo. What'd you have on the line?"

Gabriel held up one finger to indicate he wasn't finished arguing yet, and kept on edging closer to the brunette. Typical body intimidation tactics. Except she didn't seem intimidated.

"You think they'll end up in bed together?" Mitch wondered aloud.

"I'd be surprised if they managed to hold out long enough to find an actual mattress," Livi replied. Then, lifting her head and her voice, she called out, "Aunt Roz, you have a second?"

"That's about all I have." The tall woman sauntered over to hold out a hand to her niece.

"I've got a crew of hungry people here. I need to bring in another keg of beer, and somebody should pour a pitcher or three of ice over those two. And what do you need?" As always, her words ran together into one long, breathless declaration.

"I'd rather it not get out," Livi quietly told her aunt. "But I'm not sure what the stakes of this challenge were. Did you happen to hear?"

Roz's lips twitched. She gave Mitch a wink then held out her other hand for him. He eyed it, wondering if this was how the mighty felt after the fall. But it'd be rude to refuse, so he put his hand in hers and effortlessly hopped to his feet.

"Nobody seemed to have the straight of it on what the stakes are between the two of you," Roz said. "But the stakes between those two are a lip-lock versus a date."

Livi frowned.

"We tied. That means it's a draw," she pointed out. "So why are they arguing? Neither lost."

"Because Tessa says the draw means all bets are off. Romeo claims it means they both have to pay up. The money's on Romeo, if you're looking to cash in," Roz said with a laugh before heading off to do all those things she needed to do.

Mitch watched Livi as Livi watched her aunt.

And he kept watching, giving her time to work it through.

It didn't take her long. As soon as her aunt cleared the door, she turned her gaze back to him.

"So I owe you a kiss?" she asked.

"And I owe you a date," he confirmed. Mitch tilted his head toward the side door. "Shall we go discuss payment?"

STEPPING INTO THE COOL, dark storeroom ahead of Mitch, Livi flipped on the light. The bulb cast a dim glow on boxes and crates, leaving Mitch's face in shadows as he let the door shut behind him.

Livi knew she should have felt ashamed of the naughty way she'd manipulated that competition.

She didn't.

But she should have.

Her mother was fond of saying that only results counted. But having grown up *as* one of her results, Livi was just as fond of believing that actions mattered, too.

And intentions.

She leaned against a waist-high stack of crates, her eyes locked on Mitch's face as he walked toward her.

Out there in the bright room surrounded by partiers he'd seemed like a seductively sexy, extremely gorgeous, abundantly charming man. The kind of man she fantasized about.

In here he was still sexy, gorgeous and charming. But the dim shadows added an air of danger. Hinted at everything he was capable of doing. Because he was the ultimate fantasy…a SEAL.

Her excitement took on an edge that made her nervous.

What did it say about her that her anxiousness just turned her on more? He stopped a few inches away. Her pulse sped up even faster than it had during the push-ups. She tried to swallow but her throat was sandpaper.

"So, some challenge, huh?" she said, her bright words ricocheting around the room like a poorly aimed racquet-ball.

"It was interesting," he acknowledged. His eyes were like X-rays, looking so deep Livi wondered if he could see her nerves. Did they teach that in BUD/S? What other skills did he have? More than she did, for sure.

Panic pushed through her excitement.

She didn't know how to do this.

She knew how to win.

And—although some might debate it—she knew how to kiss.

But how did she handle winning a kiss?

"Interesting in what way?" she asked, desperately trying to find something clever to say, something that would keep him occupied until she figured it out.

"You play to win," he noted quietly, skimming his fingers, just the tips, down her arm from shoulder to wrist. Livi shivered, need edging aside nerves again in her stomach.

She watched his face, wishing she could see as much there as she knew he saw on hers.

"I don't do this," she blurted out. "I mean, not usually."

"Don't play to win?" He waited a beat. "Or don't play, period?"

She wanted to admit the latter. But her lack of sexual savvy had been a major bone of contention between her and Derrick—one of the key reasons for their divorce.

Any sexual shortcomings she might have were probably the kind of thing Mitch should find out for himself. After she'd found out if his mouth was as good as his body. *How's that for sexual savvy?* she congratulated herself.

His hand was still skimming, light as silk, up and down her arm. His touch was a whisper. A reminder. As if she needed one. Her body was wound so tightly she didn't know how long she could stop herself from grabbing his face in her hands and yanking that mouth to hers.

Long enough to keep from making a fool of herself, she silently promised.

"I like to win," Livi admitted. "But I don't think winning is everything."

"Heresy." His grin flashed like lightning in the dark, quick and striking. "Don't let the team hear you say that."

"You play to win?"

"I play. I win."

"You are so confident," she breathed, shaking her head

in admiration. That was almost as much a turn-on as his well-muscled body.

"I'm good."

He *was* good. He knew it and so did everyone else.

"But we drew," she pointed out. Tilting her head to the side, she wondered, "Did that bother you? Since you're used to winning, I mean?"

"I didn't lose."

"But you didn't win."

His smile was a slow seduction that meandered its way through her system with hot little licks of pleasure. It was so intense it made her nipples ache.

"Sweetheart, sometimes a draw is a win. It's all about the bigger picture. What's the real goal?"

Right now her only goal was to taste him.

Livi wet her lips in anticipation but couldn't make herself say that aloud.

"Is that one of those military things?" she asked instead. "Like sometimes losing the battle to win the war?"

"I didn't lose."

As delighted as she was turned on, Livi laughed.

He really was confident.

What was that like?

Ready to find out, she touched the tip of her tongue to her upper lip and reached out to trace her finger over the letter S on his chest.

Oh, my. He felt good. Very, very good.

She lifted her eyes to meet his, tilting her head so her ponytail swept over his hand where it rested on her shoulder.

"Super SEAL?" she asked.

"Man of iron," he promised, his hand sliding behind her neck to cup her head. Fingers tangling in her ponytail, he closed the distance between their bodies.

"Ready?" he asked, his mouth inches from hers.

"I think so," she breathed, shifting closer.

His lips brushed over hers. So soft, almost sweet.

Once.

Twice.

The third time, he added his tongue. Sliding it over the seam of her lips, along the edge of her teeth.

Livi's body flashed hot, then cold, then hot again.

Her fingers curled into his chest, the other hand grabbing his shoulder for balance.

She'd thought she was ready for this?

Oh, how wrong she'd been.

Drowning in the overwhelming sensations, Livi let herself go. Let herself feel.

And oh, my, she felt good.

His tongue danced along her lips again, then, without warning, he tightened his hand in her hair. He tilted her head back, angled his mouth and thrust his tongue inside her mouth.

His teeth scraped her bottom lip, his hands holding her head steady so he could ravage her at will. Her body went hot before everything melted into a molten puddle of pleasure.

Livi almost came then and there.

The kiss was wild.

Tongues dueled, sliding over each other in a sensual dance.

Her heart pounded in time with the fingers she kneaded against his skin. Then, wanting more, she slid her hand under the sleeve of his shirt, her fingernails scraping gently over the rock-hard delight of his bicep.

He angled closer so he was wedged between her thighs. His erection pressed against her belly, even harder than his impressive bicep.

So she did it again. This time, though, she captured his tongue between her lips and sucked while her nails skimmed from shoulder to bicep and up again.

He growled, low and deep.

She thought he'd take her.

She wanted him to.

Livi had never felt such a desperate need, such a deep, clawing desire for a man. She wanted to strip for him, to tear his clothes away. She needed to feel him, all of him, sliding over her body. Into her wet heat.

But instead of taking her, Mitch eased back.

With a long, soothing stroke of his tongue he ended the kiss, then brushed his lips over hers as if he couldn't quite bear to quit just yet.

"You blow my mind," he murmured against her cheek.

She felt his deep breath against her ear, a part of her wanting to protest that she wasn't ready for this to end. She wanted more. She needed to know what else there was.

His hands gripped her waist, lifting her so she was seated on the stack of crates she'd been leaning on.

"Oh," she breathed.

"Yeah," he agreed, moving between her thighs. His hands still on her waist, he took her mouth again.

If the last time had been a deluge this was an explosion.

Before, he'd seduced.

Now, he took.

And Livi let him.

Her hands smoothed upward along the muscles of his back before caressing his shoulders. He had incredible shoulders. His tongue played with hers, sliding then plunging, again and again.

Livi's entire being focused on his mouth. On the feel of his tongue, the glide of his lips.

Then his hands cupped her breasts.

She cried out at his touch, wet heat stabbing low and pooling between her thighs.

He didn't squeeze. Didn't rub. He just held her.

Livi squirmed, the need coiling tighter inside of her.

His mouth left hers, skimming her cheek with kisses as light as air. He nuzzled against her ear, his breath warm, before his tongue slid down her throat. Hot, wet and delicious, he buried his face in her shoulder.

Livi moaned softly, her head falling back to give him better access.

She was a woman highly in tune with her body.

She worked it, she pushed it. She made her living from it and, for better or worse, was becoming famous for it.

She thought she knew what it would do, how it would react. But as Mitch skimmed his fingers along her thigh, coming teasingly close but not touching her center, she admitted she'd had no clue.

Either that, or he was simply a superhero when it came to turning her on.

Before she could decide which, he pressed his hand against her mound, his fingers hot through the fabric of her unitard.

Livi lost it.

Oh, God.

Everything went black, tiny pinpricks of light flashing behind her eyelids as the pleasure ripped through her, tight and sharp.

Her legs tightened on his hand.

Her fingers dug into his shoulders.

Her mouth melted beneath his.

As the orgasm curled back he changed the kiss. In an instant it went from voracious to soothing as he guided her down.

It was as if he knew her body better than she did.

She'd never had an easy trigger. As much as she liked the idea of sex, she'd rarely been able to relax enough to climax during lovemaking. She hadn't relaxed with Mitch, either.

But oh, my, had she climaxed.

Fully clothed. She realized he hadn't shifted a single piece of fabric.

Livi's mind boggled.

Her body shivered.

Not just at the wonder of what he'd done.

But at the possibilities of what he could do.

"More," she breathed.

She had to have more.

DAMN, SHE WAS SWEET.

His body tight, Mitch took a deep breath and grabbed on to control. He'd known she'd taste good, but he'd had no clue she'd taste this good. Be this responsive.

His hands skimmed back up. Grazed her hips, slid over her waist, briefly cupped her breasts. Livi gave a little purr when he touched the soft warmth of her cheeks.

Her body…

He took a deep breath, blown away.

Because her body was simply amazing. Not just because she was built like his every fantasy, but because she was so amazingly responsive. He was a good lover. A damned good one. But he'd never had a woman ignite so fast, explode so intensely, then sigh so sweetly. The combination was addictive. He wanted more. He needed more.

Brushing a soft kiss over her lips, he skimmed his hands down to her shoulders, fingers sliding under her leotard straps. He wanted to push them aside. To pull them down her arms, free those breasts and look his fill.

A part of him, the part that'd been raised to be a gentleman, reminded him they were in a public storeroom and that stripping her naked—even if to worship her body—was pretty tacky.

The rest of him, led by his dick, insisted he could more than make up the tacky setting by offering incredible pleasure.

As if she sensed his internal debate, Livi shifted closer,

her tongue sliding along the seam of his mouth like hot velvet.

No question about which part he was going to listen to.

Mitch reluctantly pulled his mouth away from Livi's. She was delicious, but he wanted to watch the first time he stripped her bare.

His hands slid over her slender shoulders under the fabric. Despite the dim lighting, he could still see the slumberous excitement in her gaze, the glistening temptation of her full lips.

Before he could do more than enjoy the view, there was a loud pounding on the storeroom door.

Livi jumped. He simply turned his head toward the racket.

"Pull your pants up, I'm coming in," said a female voice.

Since his pants were secure—thanks to his hard-on, so secure he might have trouble unzipping them—Mitch didn't bother following the instructions.

He did mentally curse Romeo for losing his magical touch. In all the years they'd known each other, Mitch had never seen the guy strike out. Seriously? He had to do it for the first time tonight?

Light slanted in, bringing the racket from the party with it.

"Liv, I've got to get out of here. You want me to cab it or take your car and you can get a ride from your aunt later?"

Livi closed her eyes, gave a mortified groan and dropped her forehead onto his chest.

"Something upset her," Livi told him, her voice low so it wouldn't carry. "I should give her a ride."

Since Mitch could hear the tears in the other woman's voice, too, he could only nod and vow to get revenge on Romeo.

"I'll meet you out front in five minutes," she called to Tessa, giving Mitch an apologetic look.

He waited until the door closed, then tilted her lips up to meet his. She tasted so good.

Too good.

It was probably just as well they'd been interrupted. He didn't want their first time to have been some tacky back-room bar encounter, fast and furious against the wall. Livi deserved much better than that. But he knew he wouldn't have been able to resist her taste if she'd stayed.

"Rain check," he said against her lips.

"Okay." Livi leaned closer and traced her tongue over the join of his lips.

There came another loud thump on the door.

This time they both groaned as they separated.

"I don't think your friend is waiting out front."

"She doesn't take orders very well. But she really is upset. I should go," Livi said, her voice heavy with regret.

Mitch was tempted to ask if she always put everyone else's needs ahead of her own, but that would have been rude. And he figured one orgasm and the intention to strip her bare in a storeroom were the limits to his rudeness for the night.

So he stepped back, holding out a hand to help her down. Livi cupped her fingers around his but didn't move.

"What's wrong?" he asked.

"Will I see you again?" she asked hesitantly.

"Of course," Mitch assured her, surprised she'd asked. Not because of her stunning looks, drop-dead body and adorable personality, although those were all major factors. But because he wasn't a sleaze.

But she couldn't have known that. Mitch had to remind himself that despite how close he felt to Livi, they'd only met tonight.

"That's right." Her smile bloomed. "You owe me a date."

"That's a bet I'm looking forward to paying. But, unfortunately, I can't right away."

Ready to get her number and set up a date for the following night, Mitch glanced at his watch. And clenched his teeth as reality smacked him upside the head.

"Damn it," he muttered. At her questioning look, he grimaced and said, "I'm due on the east coast tomorrow. I have to go by the base, get my orders and catch a plane."

"Ah." Her smile was agreeable, her nod perfectly understanding. And her eyes filled with skepticism. He didn't need to be a mind reader to see her doubts, to know she'd figured he'd blow her off.

Showing impeccable timing once again, Tessa chose that moment to pound on the door.

"I guess I'll see you sometime."

He understood her suspicions. Navy guys weren't known for sticking around. Not because they were dogs, although every branch of the military had their share fit for kenneling. It was because they were deployed for long periods of time—months, years—in submarines, on ships, in other countries.

That sort of lifestyle didn't lend itself to dating, let alone to having relationships. It was irresponsible to pretend otherwise.

Mitch looked into Livi's big brown eyes and couldn't resist, though.

"I'll see you when I get back in town," he promised. "In the meantime, tell me your number."

She rattled it off.

"Aren't you going to write it down?" she asked with a frown as she slid off the crate.

"I never forget things that matter," he promised. "I'll call you when I get back."

"Will you be gone long?" she asked, her fingers rubbing the sleeve hem of his shirt so her knuckles slid over his bicep.

He wasn't going on a mission, per se. Nothing about his

trip was top secret. Still, Mitch didn't share any details of what he did. An overcautious habit, perhaps, but a habit nonetheless.

"I'll call you," he said.

Unable to resist one last kiss, he pulled her into his arms and gave himself over to whatever in the hell this was between them.

Lust. Desire. Passion or a trap, he didn't know.

All he knew was that he'd never felt anything like this before.

Mitch slowly ended the kiss, his fingers brushing her cheek before he released her.

"You're so sweet," he said with a smile. "I never realized how addicting that could be."

Then he did what he'd spent his entire life training to do.

He walked out and didn't look back.

4

LIVI'S LIPS WERE still tingling an hour later.

Tucked into her comfiest jammies, Livi sank onto her couch and sighed with pleasure. Mitch Donovan had the most incredible mouth. What else could it do? Was he a kiss-you-everywhere kind of guy? Derrick hadn't been. She had a feeling there was nowhere Mitch wasn't willing to go.

"You look like a cat with a mouthful of canary feathers," Tessa said as she brought Livi a bowl of freshly cut fruit and Greek yogurt. "So go ahead. Dish. What'd the sexy SEAL have to offer?"

Livi opened her mouth, but no words came out. Pressing her lips together, she frowned.

Between training, taping and touring, she'd spent the last year with burlesque dancers, strippers and, for a memorable couple of weeks, drag queens. All the while she'd listened to them and her crew exchange salacious stories, share intimate encounters and dish naughty details.

She finally had something worth sharing, and the words wouldn't come out.

Not for the first time she wondered what was wrong with her. Why couldn't she just put it out there, the good, the bad and the ugly? Or in Mitch's case, the incredible?

"I can't believe you were so rude," she said instead. "I've never interrupted you like that. I'm pretty sure this means you still owe me."

Tessa grimaced but didn't deny the claim.

"So you cut your flirting short," she said instead, setting

her own fruit and yogurt on the table. "It's not as if anything between the two of you had a chance of going anywhere."

"A kiss and a date," Livi reminded her.

Tessa scowled.

"You're not really going through with that, are you? It was a tie. There's no way anyone can expect you to pay double when you essentially won."

"Mitch didn't lose," Livi said, running her tongue over her bottom lip as she remembered him making that point.

"He didn't win, though. So nobody has to pay." Tessa threw her hands in the air and paced from one end of the living room to the other. Unlike Livi, she hadn't changed out of her costume. Even dressed in colorless white, she contrasted clashingly with the soothing shades of lilac and pool-blue of the room.

"Nobody?" Livi ventured. "Or you?"

Tessa stopped mid-pace, her glare hot enough to melt glass.

"Okay, what's the deal?" Livi demanded, straightening with her shoulders back and chin high. As if great posture would allow her to win the argument. "I've known you for eight years and in all that time I've seen you with hundreds, maybe thousands of men. You either seduce or freeze. You never get angry. So what's your problem with Gabriel?"

Tessa kept glaring, but Livi could tell she had to work for it. Finally, the brunette rolled her eyes.

"Thousands?"

"Sure. I count all the men I've ever seen you with. Fans, dancers, waiters. That old man who lives in the apartment below you." Livi waited a beat, then snapped her fingers and added, "The little boy who broke your window last year. What was his name?"

"Billy." Tessa's lips twitched. "I do not seduce eight-year-olds."

"Of course you do. Not sexually." Seeing that Tessa still

hadn't touched her bowl, Livi stole one of her strawberries. "But you pour on enough charm to get the guy—or little boy, in this case—to fall head over heels for you, making him so crazy he'll do anything you want."

Livi leaned forward to take a blueberry, but Tessa moved her bowl before Livi could reach it.

"What's your point?" Tessa snapped.

"My point is I've never seen you argue with a guy. Especially not a good-looking, sexy, available one. But you were right up in Gabriel's face. Why?"

Tessa's face closed up. Something flashed in her eyes, a pain Livi had seen before. But no matter how often she'd offered to listen, no matter how good of a friend she tried to be, Tessa kept whatever had caused that pain locked away tight.

"Have you met Gabriel before?" Livi couldn't help but ask.

"I know exactly what kind of guy he is. He's military. He's totally dedicated to one thing and one thing only. His career. Guys like that say they'll be back. They make all sorts of promises. But they never keep them." Tessa waved her hand through the air as if shooing away all those broken promises. "I know you think they're hot, Livi. But they belong in the look-but-don't-touch category. And more importantly, don't be touched."

Tessa gave her a questioning look.

"Oh, no. It doesn't work that way." Livi shook her head and wagged her finger at the same time. "You don't want to tell me what your issue with Gabriel is—that's your choice. But you don't get to use those issues to keep me away from Mitch."

Tessa opened her mouth. Livi leaned forward. She wondered if she'd finally find out what the hell her friend's problem with military guys was. Then the brunette snapped her teeth shut and shrugged.

"You're seriously going to date the guy?" Anger gone,

leaving her looking empty for a moment, Tessa dropped onto the pale blue couch, shifting the watercolored pillows aside. "Livi, you know I'm not big on rules. Especially not rules made by people for their good and not your own."

Livi puffed out her cheeks, knowing where this was going.

"But put aside the drama you know Pauline will create if she finds out a lowly sailor has had the gall to put his hands on her daughter, and think about her reasons for objecting."

"Mitch isn't just a sailor. He's a SEAL," Livi pointed out stubbornly. As if making it worse was going to help.

Tessa gave a look that echoed Livi's thought.

"Livi, your mom is the last person I'd defend in almost any situation *except* this one. Here, she's got a right to be biased, don't you think?"

Livi dropped her gaze to her lap, watching her fingers as they combed through the knotted fringe of her amethyst throw.

She'd grown up fatherless. The word *Unknown* had been typed in the *Father* box on her birth certificate. As far as Pauline had been concerned, Livi might as well have been conceived at a sperm bank. Actually, for quite a few years Livi had wondered if she had been. But her mother had always refused to even tell her that much.

It hadn't been until Roz had contacted her that Livi had found out anything about her father. Apparently Roz hadn't even known she had a niece until a sailor who'd happened to know her brother stopped in her bar and started reminiscing. When he'd wondered what'd ever happened to Trent's kid, Roz had gone ballistic, calling in favors and tapping sources until she'd found out.

She'd been the one to break it to Livi that her father had died during Hell Week of SEAL training. But that wasn't why Pauline felt Navy guys should be castrated right after being sworn in. It was because Trent Evans had walked out on her when she was five months pregnant to chase his dream of being a SEAL, telling Pauline that a family would only hold him back.

He'd paid sporadic child support for the first couple of months of Livi's life, but had been too focused on his goal of getting into SEAL training to bother to see her. By the time she was six months old, he'd achieved his dream of going to BUD/S, and lost his life.

Livi knew all of this secondhand. She didn't know if her mother had loved her father. She wasn't sure if they'd been together long, or what sort of relationship they'd had. She had no idea if it'd been hard on her to raise a child alone.

Pauline said life was a one-way street, and it was pointless to look backward. But for a woman who refused to discuss anything to do with the father of her child, Pauline sure spent a lot of time demanding that child make up for his sins.

Livi stared at her fingers. It was silly to be hurt over her parents' choices. They had nothing to do with her personally. She knew that, logically.

But emotionally?

Livi closed her heart against the miserable self-pity trying to take hold in it.

There was no reason for her to feel sorry for herself. She had a great career, fabulous friends and a rockin' healthy body.

And a date with the sexiest man she'd ever met.

"I can't make my decisions based on my mother's history," she told Tessa quietly. "I have to make my own history and live my own life. Don't I deserve that?"

Giving her a long look, Tessa frowned. She pulled her dented halo off and tossed it on the marble-topped table with a sigh.

"Okay, yeah. It's your life and all that." She pressed her fingers into her scalp before giving Livi a pleading look.

"But please, whatever happens, talk to me before you do anything…"

Anything what?

Sexy?

Wild?

Panty-meltingly awesome?

Too late.

"Before you do anything emotional, okay. Please."

Emotional? This from Tessa, who didn't believe emotions belonged in any room containing naked bodies? Livi almost rolled her eyes, but she could see her friend was truly worried.

"You mean emotional like falling for him and thinking we can do the happy-ever-after thing?" At Tessa's shrug, Livi shook her head. "Don't you think my divorce cured me of crazy thinking?"

"There are nice guys out there, Livi," Tessa said, looking like she wanted to kick herself. "Don't let Derrick stop you from believing in marriage and all that stuff."

As soon as the words were out, Tessa stabbed her finger toward Livi. "Except with a military guy."

"I'm not going to marry anyone, military or otherwise," Livi said with a stiff smile. "And not because my ex is an ass. I've done the marriage thing and it wasn't for me."

Livi might not have grown up in a nice, traditional family. But she'd always wanted one. A husband, children. She even thought about joining the PTA. She loved kids and had always dreamed of having one or four. She'd figured when she and Derrick had married, she had been on her way to the start of that dream. Until she'd been diagnosed with PCOS, or polycystic ovarian syndrome, and realized her chances of getting pregnant were on the "none" side of slim.

When she'd told him, instead of being heartbroken like she was, Derrick had been relieved.

He'd claimed kids would have gotten in the way of her

career, and the only marketable asset in his portfolio at the time had been Livi's body. She had it all going on, he'd said. Why ruin things?

Within a couple of months, Livi's career had skyrocketed. Her no-muss, no-fuss, bottom-line-results style of workouts was the cornerstone of Stripped Down Fitness. And people loved it. It was as if all she'd had to do was give up her dream in order to have it all. Famous clients, video deals, endorsements. Derrick had been in his element, wheeling and dealing, spending money like it was water. The higher she'd climbed, the harder she'd worked, the more he'd spent. Horrified—and yes, probably a little bitter over his emotional deceit—Livi had finally put her foot down. She'd insisted they live on a budget and invest for the future. After all, her body had betrayed her once. She had no illusions that it couldn't again.

So Derrick had walked out. He'd taken with him over five hundred thousand in investor funds and left her a pile of debt. She'd had no clue how to run her little empire.

Livi had done what any smart girl would do. She'd climbed into bed with a gallon of double-chocolate ripple and cried for a week. Then she'd called her mother. Pauline Kane knew nothing about career management. She had no connections in the fitness world and nowhere near enough money to save her daughter from financial ruin.

But she was a pragmatic businesswoman with a knack for marketing. She consigned Derrick to the bowels of hell, patted her daughter on the shoulder and rolled up her sleeves. Before Livi had recovered from the ice cream–induced gut-ache, Pauline had liquidated all of the business assets, frozen their personal ones, arranged to cosign loans to cover the repayment of investors and taken over Livi's career.

And Livi had started over.

People thought she'd been hurt by her divorce, but Livi

didn't see it that way. Her divorce had freed her, even if that freedom had carried a hefty price tag. Livi's only hurt had been in giving up her happy-ever-after dream, the one she'd nurtured since childhood. Derrick hadn't been that dream. Family had. Livi stared at her fingers as familiar grief poured through her.

Seeing it, Tessa curled her fingers over Livi's hand and squeezed.

Livi glanced up. Her friend's eyes were bright, her scowl deep. Then she took a careful breath as if she were about to impart some emotionally supportive, empowering and inspiring words.

"Derrick was a douchebag with a tiny-penis complex who deserves to be thrown under a herd of stampeding discount shoppers on Black Friday." Tessa pursed her lips then added, "While wearing granny panties."

Ah, empowerment. Livi considered that image , then blew out a breath. Couldn't argue with facts like those, either.

"See, another reason to be careful," Tessa stated. "Look at the mess Douchey Derrick left you with. I'm not saying you should avoid men. Hell, do four at a time if you want. But be, you know, emotionally careful."

Four? Where the hell did things go when there were four? Livi debated asking but decided she didn't want to know.

"It really isn't a big deal," she assured Tessa instead. And yes, maybe herself, too. "Mitch is sexy as hell and very nice. But we just met. I'm not going to do anything stupid."

"Promise?"

"Promise." Livi sealed the vow with a hug.

"Besides, I don't even know when we'd go on the date. He's leaving town for a while." She leaned back on the couch, frowning a little as it hit her what that actually meant. "The soonest I'll see or hear from him is when he gets back. And by then, who knows. He might have forgotten all about me."

The hottest guy she'd ever met.

The first one to make her forget all of her inhibitions.

The one she knew she'd be thinking of for months, if not longer.

He might forget all about the rain check, about their kiss. About her.

That was depressing as hell.

Thanksgiving
Little Creek, Virginia

"DID YOU GET ENOUGH, Mitchell?"

Enough? Mitch almost laughed. Was that possible? Had he ever tasted anything as delicious as Olivia Kane's mouth? He could feast on it for hours, days, even. The only thing more tempting than her lips was her body. It was a body made for worship. Perfection wrapped in delight coated with sweetness.

The taste of her filled his senses. If he buried his face in the gentle curve of her throat, he could breathe in her scent. It reminded him of the ocean at midnight—refreshing and cool, with overtones of mysterious danger. It'd only take one deep breath to fill his lungs before he skimmed his lips over her shoulder. Down the smooth skin of her chest before he lost himself in her body.

God, that body.

Taut muscles, generous curves.

High, lush breasts ample enough to bury his face between before he kissed his way over her firm belly. Mile-long legs corded with silken muscles, every inch of them worthy of hours of appreciation.

He wanted to start at her toes and kiss his way up those

legs, draw his tongue along her smooth thighs, then bury his head between them and lose himself in her taste.

He wanted to see that body poised over his, watch her face as he entered her, as she rode him hard, sending them both into shuddering explosions of pleasure.

Yeah.

He wanted that.

Then he wanted to do it again.

A sharp jab in the ribs yanked Mitch out of his fantasy and into the present.

"What the—?" He shot a scowl at Romeo.

And got an unrepentant smile in return. The other man tilted his head. A tiny move that silently communicated a myriad of words. *Busted*, *Pay attention* and *What's your problem?* came through loud and clear. Layered over them all was an amused sort of anticipation, as if his friend were looking forward to whatever was going to come next.

"Mitchell, are you listening to me?"

Crap.

Mitch grimaced, glancing from the forgotten fork in his hand to his plate. Sliced turkey, stuffing, vegetables, mound of mashed potatoes swimming in gravy.

Soft music created a classical backdrop to the polite murmur of voices, the rich aroma of an equally classic meal filling the air. The only-at-family-dinners-pressure of a tie around his throat intensified for a second.

Damn it, Mitch thought. Romeo was right—he *was* busted.

Mitch shifted mental gears and gave thanks that his mother served Thanksgiving dinner at a linen-covered table. It'd hide the physical evidence of his fantasy for the few extra moments it took his body to change gears, too.

Rearranging his expression, Mitch turned to offer the elegant woman across from him a conciliatory smile. As carefully presented and thoughtfully put-together as the tasteful meal and understated decor, Denise Donovan prided herself on her dinner parties. It didn't matter if it was a fancy banquet for the military brass or a quiet family dinner—she had expectations.

Mitch wasn't sure if he'd ever failed to meet them before. But he definitely had now.

"I'm sorry, Mom," he offered in his most sincere tone. "I was thinking about something else and didn't hear what you said."

"Obviously." Her eyes flashed with rare anger at her only child. It was clear she was biting her tongue to hold herself back from lecturing him on his lack of manners.

She'd have had a point.

The family's Thanksgiving dinner was probably not the best place for him to be wondering how many ways he could lick his way to the center of a very hot blonde.

Especially not with his prospective fiancée sitting right there.

His gaze shifting to the pretty brunette to his mother's right, Mitch smiled his apology. For being inattentive, he tacked on mentally. Not for the fantasy. As nice as Charity Winslow was—and even with Denise Donovan's perfect-daughter-in-law seal of approval—she wasn't his type.

Mitch knew once his mother finally accepted that, she'd give Charity a regretful hug and send her on her way. Then in the tradition that'd started somewhere around his eighteenth birthday, she'd begin her search anew.

Unlike some of the previous contenders, Charity didn't seem likely to hide naked in his bedroom, so he'd deemed it wise a few months back to make nice and put off the next round for as long as possible. With that in mind, and knowing it would go further than simply an apology to his mother, Mitch offered Charity an apology as well.

"I hear you've been busy on a new project," he added. "Is this for your own work or for your father's?"

"A little of both, actually. I've been researching physical fitness standards for grade-school children," she said, her expression pleased. "I'd love to hear your thoughts on implementing military-style fitness programs."

Mitch could just imagine a seven-year-old's reaction to his PE teacher calling him a pansy-ass and ordering him to drop and give 'em fifty. But that probably wasn't what Charity had in mind.

"I think a solid fitness regime is important, and the military gets effective results with its programs," he told her. "But I think you'd need to retool most of their methods if you wanted them to work for the average person. And even more so if you were trying to inspire children."

"I'm a machine when it comes to PT," Romeo agreed. "But it's like Irish said, I don't work as hard as I do because it's a part of my job description. I do it because I depend on my body. Because my team depends on my being in top shape. That gives me a lot more incentive than a hatchet-faced drill sergeant barking orders would."

"I don't think we'd train instructors in the art of intimidation," Charity said with a laugh. "Wouldn't good grades be enough incentive, though?"

"To do the minimum, sure," Mitch agreed. "But isn't it more important to build a love of fitness and a respect for what a healthy body can do?"

"How would you suggest doing that?"

"Games," Romeo said. "It's a tried-and-true training method in fitness and in the military."

As Romeo led everyone into an animated discussion on the various games they'd all played growing up, Mitch thought about the games he'd like to play now. His current favorite involved a telephone, a stopwatch and a challenge to see how fast he could talk Livi over the edge before he had to hang up.

His record had been set two nights ago with three minutes, twelve seconds. He was hoping to upgrade the games soon to include bare skin, body-to-body contact and a lot of sweating and moaning. He doubted the games would lead to much in the way of fitness, but Livi's body was already rock-hard. So deliciously formed. So sweet.

"Mitchell!"

Dammit. Mitch grimaced. Not again.

"Let the boy think, Denise," the Admiral ordered from the head of the table. The entire room came to subtle attention at the tone of his command. Mitch was pretty sure if the turkey could have stood and saluted a wing, it would have. "He's got a lot on his mind."

Her lips tightened in frustration before Denise pressed them into a smile for her father-in-law. After all, nobody disagreed with the Admiral.

Romeo, damn him, looked as if he could barely hold back his laughter.

"What did you think of DEVGRU?" the Admiral asked, pointing at Mitch with his forkful of turkey. "You interested?"

As he considered the question, Mitch accepted the turkey platter from his father. The platter, like many of the serving pieces, had been in his mother's family for generations. A reminder, she liked to say, of the endurance of traditions.

Mitch had always figured it had more to do with the fact that she triple wrapped each piece in Bubble Wrap and stored them in a padded case between uses. Which, he supposed, probably proved her point, too.

Traditions were as important to his grandfather, Mitch knew. Generations of Donovan men had served their country with honor. That his grandson was taking that service further than anyone else had given the Admiral plenty of bragging rights.

And he was looking for more.

"I'm not sure it's the direction I want to take," Mitch finally told the Admiral, passing the plate to Gabriel without taking any turkey. "It's an honor, of course. But I'm just as interested in the program in Coronado."

Maybe even more, considering the sweet delicacies to be found on that side of the country. But Mitch figured he'd keep that little fact to himself.

"Nonsense," the Admiral barked. "DEVGRU is the only option that makes sense."

"An option you have plenty of time to think through," his dad said from his position at what Denise liked to call the other head of the table. "A month, at least."

Thomas didn't say any more than that. He didn't need to. Four of them at the table knew he was referring to a highly classified mission Mitch was leading against a drug kingpin in Guatemala. The other two didn't need to know.

"DEVGRU? Isn't that another name for SEAL Team Six?" Charity asked in her delicate southern accent. "You're serving with Team Two right now, aren't you, Mitchell? Will your aviation training help you qualify, do you think?"

The silence in response to Charity's comment was as shocked as it would have been had she offered to perform crude sexual acts on the turkey.

Mitch and Romeo exchanged surprised looks.

Not at her comments. Charity was a congressman's aide and had obviously been well informed about the unsecured goings-on of the military. And she was clearly an intelligent woman.

But she evidently wasn't in the know when it came to social etiquette in the house of Admiral Donovan. You'd have thought that'd be one of the first things the Admiral's daughter-in-law would have schooled her protégé on.

"So," Denise said brightly before her guest could make another faux pas. "Would anyone like their drinks refreshed?"

And that's how things were handled in the Donovan house.

Mitch watched confusion, then frustration crease the brunette's face and realized this was one of the reasons he couldn't see himself getting married.

Because as much as he appreciated the family's rules on communication, he readily acknowledged that a few of them were so archaic they had chisel marks on the stone they were etched on. It wouldn't have been a big deal to say Mitch and Gabriel were assigned to one of the SEAL teams in Coronado for the next six months, or that they were currently preparing for a mission. And, hell, information on DEVGRU was readily available on the internet.

But the Admiral had strict views on the role of the support team in questioning and/or interfering with key military personnel. In other words, he expected anyone who ranked lower than O2, or lieutenant junior grade, to maintain the position of eyes down, mouth shut when it came to military matters.

"Irish can't go too far or I'll lose my excuse to come visit," Romeo told the table at large. "And we all know Mrs. D would miss me like crazy. Isn't that right, Mrs. D?"

Denise offered Romeo a smile that was equal parts gratitude and indulgence.

"Of course I'd miss you, Gabriel. But you know you're always welcome, with or without Mitchell." She shook her head in amusement at Romeo's exaggerated sigh of relief. "You are incorrigible, aren't you? How do you get better-looking each visit?"

"After all you've done to make me welcome here, the least I can do is look good for you, Mrs. D." His wink made the words a joke, but Mitch knew how serious he actually was. "What do you say we ditch these guys later and go dancing? You can teach me the real meaning of boogie nights."

Denise gave a delighted laugh and even the Admiral smiled. Nobody was immune to Gabriel's charm.

"That's enough, Romeo. Quit flirting with my wife and eat more turkey. If you don't, I'll be stuck eating leftovers for the next week."

"Aye aye, Captain."

"Mitch, aren't you going to have more?" Still smiling, his mother lifted the bowl of yams. "Charity made the yam casserole. It's your favorite, isn't it?"

"I'm still working on my first helping," Mitch admitted.

"You've got to excuse your son's poor appetite. He's developed a taste for Twinkies, Mrs. D." His face perfectly straight, Romeo gave Charity the most innocent smile he had in his repertoire. "I think the cravings might be causing him some problems today."

Mitch knew hundreds, if not thousands of creative ways to kill a man. He looked at his best friend, debating which one he'd use if Romeo didn't shut up.

"Oh, Mitchell. Twinkies are so bad for you," his mother protested. "How could you let yourself develop a taste for them?"

"Sometimes it just takes one taste," he murmured. Then he leaned forward, pitching his voice so it'd be heard by his father and grandfather. "Did you know Romeo met a woman? Totally fell for her, too."

"Gabriel, that's wonderful." Denise beamed. Her fondest hope, right after marrying off her son to the perfect woman, was marrying off all of his friends. Her theory, Mitch knew, was to surround him with so much wedded bliss that he would never catch sight of the temptations of bachelor life again.

"You finally got hooked, did you?" Thomas grinned. He didn't have his wife's hopes. He just liked seeing his son and his friends happy.

"Well, who is she? Tell us about her," Denise prodded,

slanting a sideways look at Charity. Mitch knew a trap when he saw it. But as a trained SEAL, he knew how to use it to his advantage, too.

Before Gabriel could do more than aim a deadly glare his way, Mitch offered a sad shake of his head.

"She was a sweetheart. An absolute angel. But for some reason, she didn't want anything to do with our boy here." Mitch pursed his lips before adding, "I think Romeo might be losing his touch. We might have to find him a new nickname."

The scowl on Romeo's face and the frustration in his eyes told Mitch he wasn't the only one who couldn't get Halloween out of his head. Good.

The only other person who didn't look shocked by Mitch's words was Charity. She hadn't been around long enough to understand Romeo's reputation.

"Oh, Gabriel," Denise breathed. She looked devastated, as if Mitch had just told her his friend only had hours to live.

It only took a moment for Gabriel's usual equanimity to resurface, though.

"Hey, we can't all have Twinkies," he said with a shrug and an unabashed grin.

Mitch looked from the array of delicious food spread over the table to the pretty brunette now engaged in animated conversation with his mother.

The problem was, that Twinkie was all he wanted.

5

LIVI ALMOST GOT a speeding ticket on her way to Thanksgiving dinner. Not because she was in any rush to glut on turkey. But because she'd heard her phone chime to tell her she had a text message, and she couldn't wait to stop the car and read it.

She didn't even bother to turn off the engine when she reached the restaurant parking lot. She just grabbed the first space, put 'er in park and grabbed her cell phone.

It was from Mitch. Doing a happy butt-wiggle in her seat, she read the text.

I kept fantasizing about you over dinner. You're such a distraction.

She typed back.

A good distraction?

A sexy distraction.

That's a good distraction.

I'll call later.

Livi bit her lip to keep from giggling.

She knew he couldn't actually see or hear her. But it was *so* unsophisticated. She wrote back:

Can't wait. I'll be home by ten.

Oh, my. Livi dropped her head against her seat and fanned her face. Whew. Mitch Donovan was amazing. Just a simple text from him had her all hot and excited. And three weeks after their backroom lip lock, she was still reeling.

Livi wondered if he'd seared the image of his lips on hers when he'd sent her over the edge. Or maybe her mouth was just refusing to let her forget what good kissing felt like.

Or, maybe it was his first phone call last week.

She hadn't expected to hear from him. Hoped, maybe. But not expected.

Livi had spent the week after Halloween pumping Roz for information, and the one after that tapping every resource she had on the SEALs and who knew whom.

It seemed that Lt. Commander Mitch Donovan was a wunderkind, even among the SEALs, a group known for surpassing excellence. A decorated pilot, or rather a naval flight officer, he'd trained in communications and linguistics before joining the SEALs. He'd risen through the ranks at the speed of light, in part because he kept volunteering for dangerous missions and racking up points. But smarter, Roz claimed, was that he'd trained and gotten certified in areas few others did, which meant he was in high demand.

Beyond that info, though, Livi had come up blank.

Nobody would even tell her if he was, indeed, single. If he had a girl in every port, if he left a trail of broken hearts in his wake. Or more importantly, if he liked shower sex, preferred top or bottom or was interested in including food in bedroom play.

And then he'd called. Because he couldn't resist, he'd said.

The minute she'd heard his voice, Livi had stopped caring about facts. Who needed those trivial distractions when there was sexy talk to be had? Which meant she'd asked him about showers, positions and play.

That three-minute phone call had been more exciting than actual sex with her ex had.

Of course, that had rarely lasted more than three minutes, either.

Livi hadn't asked Mitch if or when she'd see him again. She'd known he couldn't say.

But she still considered that phone call—and the handful of texts they'd exchanged since—to be perfect.

Or—she eyed the restaurant through her car windshield and sighed—perhaps it was the perfect distraction from real life. Livi grabbed the purple leather stilettos off the passenger seat and opened the car door to slide her feet in, then reached back to get her phone.

Time for family fun.

"Miss Kane," the maître d' said as she hurried in. "Let me take your coat."

"Hi, Jenson," she said, smiling as she shrugged out of the lightweight poplin. Whether it was his easy manner and the fact that he'd poured her mother into too many cabs to count, Livi always felt comfortable with the man. "Bummer that you caught holiday duty."

"It's the price we pay, isn't it," he returned with a warm smile as he took the coat. He lowered his voice conspiratorially. "And speaking of, your mother is waiting at her regular table. She's on her third Scotch."

Livi winced.

"Your aunt's only had two."

"Goody." With a deep breath and a wide-eyed look of only half-fake terror, Livi headed in.

"Wish me luck," she called over her shoulder.

His laughter followed her but unfortunately faded before she made it to the table positioned in the exact center of the room. Where better to see and be seen? Livi often wondered if her shyness was a direct response to her mother's need for attention. The more Pauline wanted it, the more Livi hated it.

"Happy Thanksgiving," Livi said optimistically, smiling at the only two relatives she had.

"Hey, sweets," Roz responded, getting to her feet and offering a hug. Her Mohawk was pumpkin-orange today, contrasting nicely with her rust-colored leather pantsuit.

Pauline didn't get up, of course. Not even the competition she considered herself to be in with the sister of her one-time lover was enough to overcome her irritation over her daughter's tardiness.

She did deign to raise her cheek for a kiss then pat the chair to her right, indicating that Livi was to sit there. The table seated five, so her daughter could sit at her elbow and leave plenty of room between her and the woman she considered to be an unwelcome interloper.

"I'm surprised it's so crowded in here," Livi observed as she slid into her seat, noting that most of the tables in the four-star restaurant were filled.

"You shouldn't be. Given the choice between slaving in a kitchen half the day and then scrubbing pots and pans, and ordering a delicious gourmet meal, I'm surprised we could get in at all."

"Tell me, Pauline. Have you ever scrubbed a pot or a pan?" Roz slanted a look over her glass of Scotch. "Or cooked, for that matter?"

Ah, it was going to be one of those dinners.

Her stomach knotting, Livi sighed and signaled for the waiter to refill the ladies' drinks. A risk, since Pauline had been known to cause a scene when she was sloshed. But unlike some people, she was more likely to throw one when fully sober. Livi cast another look around the room, hoping her mother wouldn't ruin these nice peoples' holiday.

With that hope, and her biggest smile, she leaned forward before her mother could say another word.

"It's a good thing you have a standing reservation, isn't it? Then it doesn't matter how busy it gets— you're covered."

Thanksgiving, Christmas, Mother's Day. The restaurant might change, but the tradition remained. Pauline demanded to be served. After meeting her aunt, Livi had insisted on including Roz, and Roz had come along in case she needed to step in on Livi's behalf.

"Can I get you a drink?" the waiter offered.

"A pitcher would be nice," she told him, tapping her glass. Water with lots of ice and slices of lemon. Her drink of choice at all family get-togethers.

"You should order a real drink," Pauline suggested. "We'll toast my news."

"No, I'm fine with water," Livi said. Then, because she knew it'd work better than, *I'd prefer to be sober when facing whatever you're about to spring on me*, Livi added, "Alcohol will add too many calories, and I have clients in the morning."

Livi was excited about her current mix of clients. She was working with a few new high-paying power players, two in entertainment and one in finance. Those would pay the bills and support her reputation as The Body Babe, but were insanely demanding.

In addition, she had a few dozen long-term clients that she met with several times a year to retool their workout regimes. The retooling consisted of an assessment session so she could gauge their current fitness levels and discuss their goals, a few hours of private planning in which she'd use that session's information to create a new workout regime, and a few training sessions to get them into their new groove.

And finally she had a handful of ladies who just wanted

to get in shape and, according to them, wanted the best to help them do it. They were great. The average person's reasons for getting fit were usually just as emotionally charged as the divas'. Their career might not hinge on the size of their ass, but their confidence did. She considered it a key part of her training to empower them—all of them, from the diva to the housewife.

Someday she'd be happy to shift her focus to simply coaching. But not yet. As Derrick, the genius of a businessman and snake of an ex-husband, had once pointed out, there was no money in small potatoes. That was the only thing he'd ever said that Pauline had agreed with.

"Your career is exactly what I wanted to toast," Pauline said when the waiter left again. Her eyes glittered with either triumph or battle readiness. Or, more likely, both.

Livi's stomach clenched. Pauline had given up a lot and invested so much to help Livi with Stripped Down Fitness. So Livi rarely questioned her decisions. But please, oh, please, not another tour. They'd had an agreement. Pauline had promised a reprieve until after the first of the year when her daughter had wound up the last tour. Livi wanted—needed—that entire time to gear up, recharge and get ready to kick career butt again.

"I've been pitching the idea of your own televised fitness series to a few television networks, and there's been a lot of interest. The most money is in the live option, of course, but they want a different program than Stripped Down, the prudes." Pauline laughed before she knocked back the rest of her drink.

"Television?" Livi said around the lump in her throat. "*Live* television?"

"Of course. So many stars have a regular show. You should, too. I'm holding out for a few contract changes before I accept the offer."

"Video podcasts?" Because television—live television—

wasn't bad enough? Livi took a long breath and tried to find some enthusiasm. But all that came out of her mouth was, "Why?"

"ROI, Olivia," Pauline reminded her. "It's all about Return on Investment. One-on-one sessions, videos—they take up too much of your time. You're an expert, a leader in your field. It's a waste of resources to only reach one person—or even a thousand people—at a time when you can reach millions."

When Pauline had conceived the Fit To Be Naked series, she'd said hundreds of thousands. Now she wanted millions? Livi shuddered and her stomach churned. Her breath knotted somewhere between her chest and her throat and she had to close her eyes to stop the room from spinning.

"Excuse me," she murmured as she bolted out of her seat.

Air. She needed air.

"She's fine," Livi heard her mother say as she headed for the exit. "Just a touch dramatic."

Dramatic.

Outside, not caring if it dirtied her dress, Livi leaned against the cool building and let the chilly evening air warm her terror.

Did she want to reach millions? Reaching thousands had been great, but it'd pushed her to her limits. Apparently Pauline figured the cool, impersonal lens of a camera was the perfect answer to her daughter's shyness. Livi knew Pauline was just doing as she had been asked to do. She was rebuilding Livi's brand, recouping her losses. She just had a different recouping pace than Livi was comfortable with. Because as Pauline often said, why bother with five steps if it can be done in two?

The stucco tugged at her hair as Livi rested her aching head against the building. The sooner Livi's debts were paid, the sooner she could slow down. Ready to find a middle ground, Livi lifted her chin and dusted the dirt off

EAST GRAND FORKS CAMPBELL LIBRARY

the back of her dress, then returned to the holiday festivities waiting inside. She frowned at the turkey entrée that'd been served in her absence, trying to remember if she'd actually ordered it.

"You don't give her enough credit," Roz was saying as Livi slid into her seat.

Livi sighed, wishing she could turn around and leave again.

"Believe me, I give my daughter more credit than she gives herself."

True, Livi mentally agreed as she scooped up a forkful of mashed potatoes. Mmm, real butter. Livi thought about commenting but decided she'd be better off reveling in the rich food and staying out of the hissing match.

"Livi went head-to-head with a SEAL and won."

"I beg your pardon?"

The butter stuck in Livi's throat.

Oh, hell.

Heads turned at Pauline's icy tone. Livi wanted to take her food and crawl under the table.

Or better yet, right back outside.

"It was a tie," Livi muttered before facing her mother, ready to appease. "And it was nothing, really."

Pauline's face was turning the same purple as Livi's skirt. It didn't look nearly as good on her, though.

"Nothing?" Roz hooted. "You drew in a push-up competition with a SEAL. Believe me, nobody does that. Especially not against that particular SEAL."

Stop. Please, don't say anything else. Eyes wide, Livi tried to send her aunt the message. Roz knew Pauline's prejudice against all things Navy and SEAL. But Roz was too busy trying to score points to pay Livi any attention.

"Olivia?" Her mother's look could have sent Jack Frost running for a sweater. "Is this true?"

Before Livi could answer, Roz leaned forward, stabbing

her turkey-loaded fork in the air. "Someone issued a challenge and she stepped up, met it and kicked butt. There aren't many men who can compete against a SEAL. But Livi did."

Most men didn't flirt and use sexual innuendo against SEALs, either.

"You entered a fitness challenge against one of the Navy's best?" Pauline said slowly, looking to Roz for confirmation instead of Livi.

"Best of the best." Roz nodded. Then, realizing she'd thrown her niece under a bus, she added, "All Livi did was help me out after these guys challenged her. You know how they can be. What's a girl to do except kick some butt?"

Kick some butt? Livi almost laughed out loud. She remembered grabbing some butt—and a very nice butt at that. But she didn't figure her mother needed to know that.

She wiped the amusement off her face when Pauline glanced her way, her pale blue eyes assessing the situation.

"You beat a SEAL in a straight push-up challenge?" she asked.

"It's no big deal. Why don't we eat before the food gets cold?" Livi suggested, lifting her fork. "Delicious gourmet Thanksgiving food, remember?"

"Let me finish thinking this through."

Oh, no. She knew that look. It was her mother's "how can we make this molehill into an attention-grabbing mountain" look.

Livi had a lot to be grateful to her mother for. Her career was kicking fitness butt thanks to Pauline's vision and drive. And Livi loved that. But, damn it, she was still so worn-out. For an introvert to spend over a year touring and meeting people was a lot. For a shy introvert? It was a dance through hell. She'd done it once. She could—would—do it again. But she had to recharge first.

"I'm on hiatus," she reminded her mother. "No new projects until next year, remember?"

"Darling, you know I never break a promise." Her smile edged with calculation, Pauline reached over to take Livi's hand. "But we need a new focus. A way to reach the top. This could be it."

"I thought we'd had it with the Fit To Be Naked program." She didn't mention the television deal. Hey, if that'd fallen off Pauline's radar, she wasn't about to bring it up again.

"Fit To Be Naked got you noticed, darling. And the projected earnings are fabulous. But now is the time to capitalize on your rise, not to relax." Pauline patted her hand. "You wouldn't train for a marathon then take a week's vacation before running it, would you?"

Maybe. It depended on what was waiting for her at the finish line.

"The SEALs' fitness program is famous. It's one of the most sought-after in the country," Pauline mused, turning to Roz. "I researched it when I was looking for markets for Olivia. Hundreds of trainers offer what they call a SEAL workout, but they're usually based on supposition."

"Bet you'd get a lot more traction if you had SEAL input," Roz chimed in, sliding her turkey through the gravy.

Livi was pretty sure this was the first time she'd seen her mother and aunt make nice with each other.

"You want me to develop a SEAL workout?" Livi asked slowly, not wanting to say anything that'd mess with the tentative peace.

"I think it's worth looking into." Pauline nodded.

"Our girl here can probably tap a SEAL herself and get some info." Seeing Livi's frantic, if tiny, shake of her head, Roz quickly added, "Or you know, I can pull some strings, see if I can get some inside info on their actual training."

Grateful, Livi sipped her water. Then it hit her like a bolt of lusty lightning. This was another way to connect with

Mitch. Excitement swirled in her belly, her pulse doing a little happy dance.

"Well, then," Pauline said, lifting her glass in a toast. "It looks as if we have a fun new project for the New Year."

Livi almost did a happy dance herself, right there in the middle of the restaurant.

She couldn't wait until January first.

MITCH STRODE DOWN the hall to Captain Tilden's office, wondering about his order to report immediately. He couldn't imagine what Public Affairs wanted with him. He and the team had completed their mission three days ago and finished debriefing the previous one—nothing that'd merit a press release. If there had been anything else PR-worthy, Mitch knew his grandfather would have filled him in. The Admiral had headed back to Virginia after the debriefing, leaving orders for Mitch to follow before Christmas Eve. That order, the Admiral had added, had come from Denise, who would withhold his Christmas pudding if her son weren't in attendance.

Apparently there were occasions when a mother just had to buck protocol.

With almost two weeks before he had to make that appearance, Mitch planned to put his time to good use. He had to collect on a bet. He'd only talked to Livi once since Halloween, but her phone number was etched in his memory. He was looking forward to using it.

He had been too well trained to let thoughts of her distract him from the job at hand. But Mitch had drifted off to sleep each night remembering the taste of her.

He knew Romeo would claim that those bedtime memories proved Mitch was addicted. But Mitch figured it was just the opposite. It'd been six weeks since he'd tasted her, and he'd managed to contain his thoughts all that time.

He deserved a reward.

And he'd get it tonight.

Today he was diving into vigorous obstacle training. The team needed to work off the adrenaline from the mission before they shifted back to the tactical flight command training he was in Coronado for. He'd been leading the team in a belly crawl over the sand, each man carrying a fifty-pound log on his back, when the order to report came in.

Now he had to find out why.

Mitch stopped outside the captain's office, took off his cap and beat it against the leg of his fatigues to knock off the sand. Then he put it back on and stepped through the door.

Standing out like a sore thumb was the tiny potted evergreen decorated with glittering anchors and miniscule sailors' caps. Utilitarian gray with a glittering candy cane broach, Tilden's secretary was a perfect match for the sparsely furnished office. She glanced up from her keyboard when he entered and tilted her head to the other door.

"He asked that you go right in," she instructed in a gravelly voice.

Deciding that Tilden must do most of his public relations on the internet or at lunch, Mitch knocked to announce his arrival, then stepped into the room.

The first thing that hit him was a scent.

The ocean at midnight.

Livi?

"Mitch Donovan. What a pleasure."

Brow creased at the greeting, Mitch looked around the room. The only person there was Captain Tilden. The guy was his grandfather's age, but unlike Admiral Donovan's air of dignified leadership, Tilden's air was that of a happy hippo. Wide-faced, with jowls that had a mind of their own, the guy hefted himself out from behind the desk and came forward with his hand out.

His own hand halfway to a salute, Mitch quickly

changed directions and shook Tilden's hand. He surreptitiously sniffed to see if the guy was wearing Livi's perfume.

Nope. Just cheap cigars and—Mitch sniffed again—was that roast beef?

"Sir," Mitch said, feet planted hip distance apart, hands clasped behind his back. "Donovan reporting as ordered."

"I don't stand on ceremony in here. Go ahead, take a seat," the man suggested, as he did the same.

Once Mitch sat, the captain tapped his fingers on his desk twice and smiled.

"Our office has been asked to accommodate a media venture. The SEALs workout program is one of the most sought-after, as you know. The press is all over it. Hundreds claim they are teaching it. Everyone wants a piece. It's like they think if they can do a SEAL workout, they're hot shit."

Mitch waited a beat, not bothering to react. He knew Tilden was trying to get a rise out of him. But Mitch had trained as a green ensign under some of the toughest recruit division commanders in the Navy. Until the pudgy cigar puffer across the desk found a ruder way to insult Mitch's mama, one that included ocean life, twenty sailors and a cannon, he wouldn't even come close to riling Mitch up.

"How does this apply to me?" Mitch finally asked. He could see how they could *make* it apply, but he'd have liked to be wrong.

"You're the man," Tilden said, cocking his finger like a gun and pulling the trigger. "Big SEAL on campus, so to speak. You'll be the go-to guy for this project. The public face."

"Wouldn't someone else—" *anyone else* "—be better suited for this? One of the BUD/S trainers, for example."

"The orders came down from on high, my friend. Special request. You are the golden boy and they want you in the limelight. Might have something to do with that brand-spanking-new promotion you got, Commander."

And there it was. The reason the Captain was acting like a dumbass. Well, Mitch considered, looking the guy over, one of the reasons. Mitch had dealt with plenty of that in his years of service. The judgment, the speculation, the jealousy. It was a lot easier for some guys to believe that nepotism, favors and ass-kissing had played into Mitch's swift rise through the ranks than to accept the fact that he was simply one of the best.

"What are the orders?" Mitch asked calmly. No point engaging an idiot. Besides, he knew his demeanor only irritated guys like Tilden.

He knew he was right when the older man's smile dipped into a brief sneer before he got control of his face again.

"Take the visitor on a tour, outline the BUD/S training and give a few glowing details of how hard you SEALs keep working to stay fit." Tilden's wink made him look like a leering hippo rather than a happy one. He patted a folder on his desk. "We won't share our current training program, of course. I've pulled together a basic dossier of authorized responses as they relate to the subject matter and of details of the previous program that you're authorized to share."

He paused before adding, "I'm sure I don't have to remind you of the importance of confidentiality in this matter."

Seriously? Since when was fitness fraught with secrecy?

Mitch wasn't about to ask. Especially considering he'd probably surpassed the captain's security clearance about five years back. Mitch had served countless missions, completed a myriad of assignments in his decade in the military. But he couldn't remember one like this. Maybe it was connections—it'd be naive to think nepotism had never touched his career. Or maybe it was having served under intelligent leaders who recognized the correct use of the tools under their command. Whatever it was, it was sure missing right now.

"Your liaison is waiting in the visitor's center."

Accepting the dismissal and the dossier, Mitch got to his feet.

"The objective is in the file? The contact's company profile?" Mitch couldn't hold back his scowl when Tilden shook his head. "A name?"

"Sorry, Donovan. This didn't come through regular channels, so I have limited specifics. But hey, you're a SEAL. I'm sure you can handle a fluff assignment like this."

It only took three seconds before Mitch's hard stare wiped the smirk off the Captain's face. The older man got to his feet, his fingers tapping his desk next to his phone.

"Anything else, sir?" Mitch asked, his tone low and deadly. More because he wanted to amuse himself than because he was irritated. It was pointless to waste energy on guys like Tilden.

"Dismissed."

Mitch executed a neat about-face and marched out the door. He didn't slow down or relax his posture until he was halfway to the visitor's center. He gave a quick glance at the dossier with its dearth of information and frowned. There wasn't even a reporting officer listed.

Sloppy work. Mitch glanced back toward Tilden's office and shook his head. At least he didn't have to go into battle with the guy.

Mitch folded the file and stuffed it into his back pocket, then pulled open the door to the visitor's center.

Looked like he'd be doing some recon along with PR.

He stepped into the visitor's center and was hit with that scent again.

The ocean at midnight.

Mitch's mouth watered.

His body went rock-hard.

Livi.

6

IT WASN'T HARD to find her.

Besides the civilian manning the desk, she was the only person there. Even if the room had been packed with people, he'd have seen her. She was impossible to miss.

Once in battle, Mitch had taken a blow that'd sent him over the edge of a cliff. He had the same dizzy, mind-bending feeling then as he did right now.

Livi.

Her hair was loose today, flowing in blonde waves across her forehead, over her shoulders to the tips of her breasts. She wore a little red suit, but she'd have glowed just as brightly in burlap.

"Mitch." With a wide smile, she unfolded herself from the chair, those mile-long legs uncrossing as she straightened and stepped forward. "Hello."

Mitch's mouth went dry.

From the toes of her shiny black shoes, which were straight out of his most embarrassing dreams, to the flash of red in her earlobes, she screamed class. He ran his gaze up, then down again, taking in the skirt that showed enough leg to cause a traffic accident. Up to her fitted jacket, snug at the waist and edged in black. Sexy class.

Livi dressed in spandex and sponge cake had been adorable. The kind of woman he could laugh with before sliding into playfully delicious sex.

Livi of the rock-hard body he'd watched on video had been impressive. The kind of woman who'd challenge him to prove his manhood in very erotic ways, all of which would have required them to be naked.

But this Livi?

This Livi was confidently sexy. She looked like a woman he could take home to meet his family. Even more, she looked like the kind of woman his mother was always bringing home to meet him. Like one who'd help his career. Who'd mingle with the brass, hold her own with their wives and charm everyone she met.

That shouldn't have turned him on.

But somehow it did.

Or maybe it was the shoes again.

"Are you here to see me?" he asked, taking her hand in his and slowly pulling her closer. Not close enough to give the civilian manning the desk anything to talk about. But close enough for Mitch to breathe in her scent. To feel her warmth and see the delight in her eyes as they widened at his move.

"I am indeed here to see you, Commander Donovan," she said, her smile widening. "And congratulations."

"Are you congratulating me on your visit?" he teased, his fingers sliding over her slender wrist. He could feel her pulse racing at a gratifying pace. But there was no anxiety in her eyes, no worry in her smile. Which left excitement.

"I'm congratulating you on your promotion," she said with a laugh. "But if you'd like, you can consider my visit a part of that congratulations."

"I think I might." Reluctantly, he released her hand, sliding his fingers along her wrist and over her palm, skimming her fingers as her hand slid away.

And grinned when her breath hitched a little.

"I'm also here to get your input into the new fitness program I'm developing," she said in a husky tone.

Yeah. He'd figured that.

"Why don't we go somewhere where we can talk." He slanted a glance at the now-staring clerk. "Privately."

"Do you have a storage room handy?" she asked, her words low enough that only he heard them.

He also felt them with the same intensity as he would have if she'd run her tongue down his body.

Seeing the heat in her big brown eyes, the sensual curiosity in their depths, he changed his mind. Her words were a turn-on, but he was sure her tongue was pure magic.

"Why don't we start with an office," he suggested, tilting his head toward the door. She stepped around him, offering him a mouth-watering view of her backside. The red fabric hugged, slid, tempted. Mitch hurried forward to open the door for her, hoping he didn't have drool on his chin.

As soon as they stepped into the weak December sunshine, he added, "I'll see what I can do to find one with crates."

Her eyes widened then she burst into laughter. The sound turned heads. The heads stayed turned out of appreciation as people caught sight of how gorgeous she was with the sun glinting off her hair.

He'd thought he'd been excited about calling her again. He'd known he was looking forward to seeing her again.

But obviously he'd had no clue how strongly he'd want her, crave her—God help him, need her.

And that was after just one look.

What would he feel after he'd spent more time with her? Gotten to know her? Tasted, touched and buried himself in her?

He couldn't wait to find out.

RELIEF POURING THROUGH her with enough intensity to make her lightheaded, Livi took a good, deep breath for the first time in two days. Ever since her mother had told her she'd gone ahead with the SEAL workout idea, Livi had been worried. They'd agreed that they'd discuss it after the New Year. She'd figured that would give her time to talk to Mitch, to make sure he was okay with it. But when she'd spoken with him after Thanksgiving, she'd chickened out. He'd said he'd be out of touch, which she'd taken to mean he'd be off doing intense SEAL things. She hadn't wanted to waste their little bit of time on that when it was so much more fun to ask him what he was wearing. She'd do it during the next call, she'd promised herself, sure there would be at least one before the New Year.

She slid a sidelong glance at Mitch, grateful to see he didn't seem put out by her visit—or the reason behind it. Seeing her look, he offered that warm smile of his and Livi forgot her worries. She almost forgot her name.

He was just so yummy.

Livi was a woman gifted with a vivid imagination. So vivid that it sometimes overruled her memories, painting them with a much rosier hue than the reality had been. So she'd wondered if she'd built Mitch up to be better-looking and sexier in her mind.

As he led her across the compound toward a bank of low buildings, she kept sneaking glances at him. Her appreciative gaze took in the breadth of those amazing shoulders, the chiseled perfection of his biceps and the slender angle of his waist as it tapered beneath his simple blue T-shirt.

His cap, the same blue as his eyes, cast a shadow over the upper part of his face. But that only served to highlight his mouth. Oh, what a mouth.

Livi almost tripped over her own feet, she was so distracted by the memory of how tasty that mouth had been.

"You okay?" Mitch's fingers tightened on her elbow.

"Mmm," she murmured, shifting her eyes forward to watch where she was going.

Yes. She definitely had a vivid imagination.

But her imagination had nothing on the reality of Super Hottie.

Her brows rose at the sight of a dozen men jogging past in shorts and tanks, each one a testament to the sexiness of fitness. As they passed, she noticed they were all soaked, as if they'd just come out of the ocean. Despite her appreciation of the view, she shivered a little.

"Cold?" Mitch asked.

"No, but I think I would be if I were them." She tilted her head to indicate the column of men that'd now passed. "I know we have good weather, but December is a little chilly for swimming, isn't it?"

"Sea Air Land—that's what SEAL stands for and that's where we train. Weather doesn't matter." His eyes amused, he gestured to a path angling to the right. "If I were still in Virginia, we'd be doing the same workout."

"Doesn't it snow there?"

"Weather doesn't matter," he repeated.

Another group passed, these men all wearing white uniforms, complete with caps. Livi smiled at them and one or two smiled back, while the rest kept their eyes forward.

"This is like a movie set," she realized as she glanced around. "One of those wonderful black-and-white ones with moody background music and a tragic opening scene."

"Starring the prerequisite femme fatale in a tight skirt?" He glanced at hers and gave an appreciative smile. "Looks like you'd fit the role."

Delighted both at what she took as a compliment and at the fact that he'd watched enough old movies to appreciate the genre, Livi put a movie star oomph into her step.

"Yeah, you'd definitely fit the role," Mitch murmured with an appreciative smile.

"I'd need a very charming, very sexy leading man," she decided, tapping her finger against his bicep. It was all Livi

'He's shy," Gabriel explained with a shrug, his expres
making it clear that even though he knew the wor
really didn't understand the concept.

But she *definitely* understood. Livi sent a sympathet
ile toward Scavenger's retreating back. Poor guy.

"Why don't you go help him work through that issue
itch suggested pointedly. Arms crossed over his che
e gave Gabriel an arch look.

Which Gabriel deliberately ignored.

"Nah, he's fine." Shifting his weight a little so his shou
der was toward Mitch, Gabriel gave Livi a brilliant smi
"So, gorgeous, how've you been? And even more imp
tantly, how is your angelic friend?"

Amused, Livi shifted a little bit toward Mitch to inclu
him in the conversation.

"Tessa is great," she said. "She'll be sorry she miss
seeing you."

His expression woeful, Gabriel shook his head a
sighed deeply enough to bring his shoulders into the ac

"Now, see, you need to practice lying. You say the wo
right, but that sweet innocent face of yours tells a diff
nt story."

"And what story is that?" Livi asked, laughing.

"Angel is a complicated woman," he told her, droppi
voice as if he were sharing a secret. "She's as compl
she is gorgeous. Smart, sexy, savvy and seductive. E
ly, she's missing something."

"As her best friend, I might be inclined to agree w
r assessment if I knew what you think she's missing
Me." He smiled, that devastatingly gorgeous face lig
efore he winked. "Now, I hate to do it because I kn
much Irish wants me to stick around. But duty cal
e got to go."

gave Livi a friendly hug, punched Mitch in the sho

could do not to give a long hum of approval. "A big, hand-
some SEAL determined to save the world."

"The whole world?"

"Sure, why not?" she said with a laugh, waving her hand
to indicate everything around them. "This seems like a
saving-the-world kind of place."

"Is this your first visit to the naval base?" he asked, guid-
ing her into one of the larger buildings.

Livi hesitated, not quite sure how to answer. She'd vis-
ited the naval base once before in an attempt to meet her
grandfather. But she'd never made it out of the visitor's
center.

Thankfully, before she could figure out if she should
share that or not, they came face-to-face with a group of
men who had clearly just finished an extreme workout.

"Oh, my," she said quietly, appreciating the view as only
a woman devoted to fitness could. It was like seeing her
professional Holy Grail.

Muscles gleamed and rippled beneath their damp
T-shirts, all of them exuding the sort of energy that came
from intense physical exertion. Livi wanted to bottle that
energy up and take it with her to show clients just why
they should push their bodies.

Even better, she'd like to take the men. If they didn't
inspire a woman to want to feel her best, Livi didn't know
what would.

"Yo, Donovan. We thought you deserted." The speaker
was roughly the size of a house, his red hair shaved in an
old-fashioned flattop.

She felt the subtle change in Mitch.

He didn't move. His expression didn't change. He simply shifted his stance. As soon as he did, the group qui-
eted, settled.

Command, she realized. He didn't question it and neither
did his men. But every one of them respected it.

"Livi, meet…" His words trailed off as the men made a show of jostling each other out of the way to get to the front of the group.

Livi bit her lip to keep from giggling. Mitch shook his head then waved a hand to address the entire group.

"Meet part of the team," he said. "Gentleman, this is Olivia Kane. She's here to discuss our fitness program."

"Best in the world," one man said.

"Ain't nothing like it," another added.

Suddenly the crowd was made of people who expected her to converse instead of impressive examples of fitness devotion. Butterflies danced through Livi's stomach, making it hard to breathe for a second.

Common ground, she reminded herself as she took a deep breath. Just focus on common ground.

"Everything I've heard says you're definitely the best," she agreed with her brightest social smile. "I've studied similar programs and spent a week training with a former Green Beret, but even he said your program is impressive."

"You trained with a Green Beret?" the redhead asked, looking her up then down, as if trying to figure out how.

"While I was getting my ACSM certification," she confirmed. She'd taken extensive courses with him later as well, but mentioning that would probably be considered bragging. It hit her that she really wanted Mitch to know her qualifications. To realize she was serious about her career—dedicated to being the best she possibly could.

Before that need overruled her hesitance to brag, a voice called from the back of the crowd.

"Whose ass do I have to kick to get out the door?"

A few guys laughed and a few others shifted to open a path for the speaker. Tall and lean, his short black hair gleamed almost as much as his golden skin did.

When he saw Livi his eyes flashed to Mitch for just a moment before he offered her a grin.

"Well, well. I knew you were the type t

"Gabriel," Livi greeted with a smile, ho hands to take his. "How are you?"

"Who?" muttered the redhead.

"Gotta mean Romeo."

"You talking about Thorne?"

Gabriel rolled his eyes, but otherwise ignore ters.

"Hit the showers," Mitch ordered quietly, an expression on his face.

Before Livi could blink, the crowd was gone. F large men, they moved incredibly quickly. Only o mained, a tall, lean guy with sea-green eyes too dr to belong to a military man.

"They don't know your name?" she asked Gabriel.

"We're new," he explained. "It takes some teams a wl to decide if they want to be on a first-name basis or not

"I thought you'd been here for a while," Livi said didn't have to count backward to Halloween. The weeks had been marked with tally marks in the l her mind.

"Time's relative." Gabriel shrugged. He tilted to indicate the quiet man next to him. "Besides, Ir enger and I have been here, there, everywhere loween—"

"Why don't you meet us tomorrow?" Mitch "You can fill Livi in then on the intricacies of among the men."

Gabriel rocked back on his heels with a his head toward the man next to him and Scavenger. I think Irish might be trying t

"Sounds like he's trying to get rid of yo said with a fleeting smile. "Me, I'm alre

With a polite nod, he murmured *"Ni Livi. He gave Mitch a modified finger-

der and headed out the door. Before he went through, he tossed over his shoulder, "You tell Angel she still owes me."

"She'll be thrilled," Livi deadpanned.

"That's the thing about Romeo," Mitch told her, gesturing to a door on the right. Since half of the wall was glass, she could see it led to an empty room. "He always collects."

"Then this should get interesting." Livi brushed against him when she crossed the narrow hallway, her shoulder skimming his chest. Just the lightest touch of his body, with layers of fabric between them, and she felt heady with excitement. Who knew what'd happen if he kissed her again.

Given how much she'd thought about it over the last seven—yes, of course she'd counted—weeks, she was pretty sure the touch of his tongue on hers would inspire yet another orgasm.

She was more than willing to test the theory, too.

"We'll have at least a semblance of privacy in here," Mitch said, gesturing for her to precede him through the door. Livi stepped in and wondered if she should have left her purse behind so they both could fit.

"Snug," she said with a smile, angling her tall form into one of the two metal chairs framing a small table.

Mitch didn't sit. Instead, he leaned one shoulder against the closed door, his arms crossed over his chest and one ankle over the other.

"So... The Body Babe is looking for fitness advice from the SEALs?"

Livi tried to laugh despite her sudden discomfort, but all she managed was a smile.

"I hope you don't mind," she said, clasping her hands in her lap as she leaned forward. "I know you weren't expecting to see me yet, and definitely not under these circumstances."

"Why don't you tell me how these circumstances came

about," he invited. He didn't sound angry or even annoyed. Simply curious.

Livi wet her lips, wondering if anyone could actually be that even-tempered and confident. She knew she hadn't seen a lot of Mitch, but their meetings had both included situations that she realized were likely to at the very least irk another man. Being beaten—draw or not—by a woman at a physical contest never sat well. But Mitch had only smiled and done an incredible, orgasmically impressive job of paying his bet. And now this?

Livi pursed her lips and considered. Maybe if they spent enough time together, some of his confidence would rub off on her. She'd have to rub against him as much as she could, just in case. Or, at the very least, watch and see if she could learn any tips.

"These particular circumstances came about because Roz was bragging about Halloween, and one thing led to another. Before I knew it, my manager was brainstorming a new video idea and Roz was calling in favors," Livi explained with an apologetic shrug. "I figured it'd take them until the first of the year at the earliest to put something together, and by then I'd have had time to talk to you in person."

"I'm impressed your manager was able to pull it off. A lot of people have tried, and the usual response is no." His smile flashed with charm. "I'd love to know whose buttons they pushed."

Livi had asked, but she still didn't know who Pauline or Roz had contacted in order to pull this off.

"My manager can be a bit aggressive," she said instead, offering the understatement with a grimace. "I hope this isn't a problem."

She waved her fingers in the air to indicate her, him, the situation, everything.

"A problem seeing you again?" Mitch's smile widened,

deepened with a warmth that lit an answering heat low in Livi's belly. "You're kidding, right?"

"And discussing the program with me?" she asked hesitantly.

"Orders are orders," Mitch said with a shrug. "I was instructed to assist, and I'm here to do just that."

Livi couldn't tell how he felt about it, but at least he didn't look angry.

"So what do you need?" he asked.

"Advice, insights, general guidelines," she elaborated. "I'm happy with anything you'd like to offer."

His blue eyes darkened for a moment, as if he were imagining other offers that might make her happy.

More than ready to get the official stuff out of the way so she could find out what he had in mind, Livi flipped open the clasp on the black, patent leather cylindrical purse and pulled out a notepad and pen. Then she gave him an expectant smile.

"Okay, shoot."

A half hour or so later, Livi had filled over a dozen pages with notes, a few sketches and a couple of diagrams. She'd gone over the file Mitch had been instructed to share and clarified training phases—recovery and regeneration, adaption and plateaus.

Flipping through the pages, she felt a little giddy. The way some women did in a shoe store or others did when cruising through Tiffany's. It was a bone-deep appreciation with a little zing of avarice and a whole lot of sexy thrown in.

"Can I see your gym?" she asked, looking up from her notes.

Mitch's indulgent smile dimmed for a second, then he shrugged. "Sure."

Livi could tell he wasn't crazy about bringing her into man-land. She wasn't surprised. Some men were territorial about their workout space. Used to the attitude, Livi kept to the edges of the gym, making sure she didn't step onto the actual workout floor. She didn't let her eyes rest on any one of the dozen or so exercising men for more than a second, and she kept her body language unobtrusive.

But she saw everything.

"My, you have some nice equipment here," she said quietly, doing her best Tessa impression, complete with husky voice, slumberous eyes and wicked laugh.

"You should see me use it," he shot back with an appreciative smile.

Livi's breath caught, her body tingling at the very thought. Oh, my, she'd love to see that.

She shot one last look around the gym, noting the glances being sent their way. It was easy to read the thoughts of the dozen or so men in the room. She was an intruder and in true military fashion, they wanted the intruder gone.

"Thanks for showing me around," she said, making her way to the exit. She waited until they'd left the gym before giving him a grateful smile. "I would love to do the actual workout here sometime."

His gaze took a long, slow journey over her body, leaving desire in its wake. "You aren't really dressed for a workout."

His eyes met hers again with a look so hot Livi's thighs trembled. Heat, wet and sticky, pooled between them in anticipation of that look's promise.

"You'd be amazed at what I can work out in," she said, remembering a few workouts with the strippers she'd toured with.

"Is that a fact?" His smile was a little wicked. "Are you so dedicated that you wear workout gear under your clothes?"

Livi wet her lips and gave him a look from beneath her lashes. Even though they were back in the broom closet of an office, she still dropped her voice to a low purr.

"All I'm wearing underneath are a couple of teeny, tiny scraps of silk." She waited a beat, reveling in the desire lighting his eyes. "I don't think they'll offer much support if we get very active."

His eyes dropped to her chest, as if assessing just how much support she needed. She almost groaned as she imagined him reaching up to cup her breasts, testing their weight in his palms. He had such big hands.

Big, strong, talented hands, she'd bet.

Without thinking, she reached out to take one in hers. Holding it between them, she traced the index finger of her other hand along his palm, delighting in the hardness.

"You have clever hands," she murmured. "Working hands. The kind that can handle anything."

Her eyes met his, her body reacting instantly to the heat in those blue depths.

"Hands like these might not be able to handle teensy pieces of silk," she teased.

"You'd be amazed," he said quietly, his gaze molten.

Livi's heart thumped so hard she was surprised it didn't leap out of her chest and land at his feet. Her pulse jumped right along with it, edgy desire grabbing her. Making her want. Making her need.

Then, in a blink, his gaze was friendly again. He released her hand, leaving Livi standing there with her notes and a whole lot of lust.

"So," he said, drawing out the word until she'd closed the notebook and met his eyes. "You have everything you need?"

For her interview about the SEAL workout? Yes.

Personally? Livi was pretty sure she needed a whole lot more now than she'd ever realized she could.

But that wasn't what he was asking about, she reminded herself.

"Thank you so much for the wonderful information,"

she said. Thrilled with her extensive notes, her mind raced with ideas for modifying the compound exercise combinations and functional routines to make them accessible for people at different fitness levels.

"Then we've handled our business?" He sounded so official it was easy for Livi to imagine him directing troops and issuing orders.

"I think so," she said slowly. Was he going to kick her out?

"Then it's time I took a clue from Romeo."

"I'm sorry?" Livi frowned.

"Our bet."

"Oh." Delight, purely feminine, partially sexual, filled Livi as she smiled. "I've already collected my prize."

"How about I collect mine tonight? Dinner?" he suggested, still using that distant tone.

Her heart leaped, but she still hesitated. Silly, since she'd been looking forward to their date for over a month. But nowhere in her imagination had she forced him to see her beforehand.

Whether he'd read her mind or simply had a busy schedule, Mitch glanced at the clock hanging on the steel-gray wall.

"I was going to call when I got off duty today to see if you'd like to go out."

"Then I'd love to go to dinner tonight," she agreed, probably much too eagerly.

"I need to shower and change." His words were said in a husky whisper.

"Do you want me to wait for you?" she offered, not sure she could. Her body was wound so tightly, all it would take was a touch, just the hint of his finger trailing over her bare skin, to make her explode.

"Why don't I meet you at your place?"

7

A DATE, A DATE, oh, goody, a date.

The chant accompanied her all the way home. It played in her head as she emailed her mother a quick report stating the meeting had gone well. She hummed it as she hurried through the apartment, tidying.

As she plumped pillows, she wished she'd thought to stop for fresh flowers.

Oh, God, a date.

She hadn't been on a date in years. Unless going out with Derrick while they'd been married counted, and she really hoped it didn't. The most fun she'd had on those dates was beforehand, when she got to pick out an outfit.

An outfit.

Livi dropped the barely plumped pillow and ran for her bedroom, stripping as she went. Her shoes flew toward the foot of the bed as her fingers made quick work of the buttons on her jacket.

What was she going to wear?

Mitch hadn't said if he was taking her someplace dressy or casual. Did she wear sequins or denim? Heels or flats? She didn't want to overdress, but underdressing was just as bad, wasn't it?

She tossed her jacket on a chair and shimmied out of the skirt. Standing in the middle of her walk-in closet wearing nothing but the tiny bits of silk she'd mentioned earlier, Livi flipped through hangers so fast, the fabric was a blur of color. Every once in a while she paused to consider.

A simple black skirt with a silk tee was casual enough,

but could be dressed up quickly by adding her fat black pearl necklace. But it was more businessy than sexy.

Back to flipping hangers.

Her little red slip dress was definitely sexy, but the brushed cotton, if paired with flat sandals, would dress it down. The hanger was halfway off the rod when Livi remembered it was December. Back it went. The flipping resumed.

She'd finally narrowed her choices to a sheer black blouse with poet sleeves that she could pair with a red cami and skinny jeans, or a nubby silk sheath in khaki with a matching jacket. Wait. Wasn't khaki more an Army color than a Navy one? Livi started flipping hangers again. Then she found the perfect dress.

A white crocheted minidress with cap sleeves and a scooped neckline. She'd pair it with her nude peep-toed sandals.

When the doorbell rang, she started, almost sending the dress into orbit. She glanced at the clock and grimaced. It was too soon for Mitch. She hoped it wasn't Tessa wanting to hang out. Or worse, her mother, here for a more detailed report on the meeting. Livi grabbed her robe, a swirling column of watercolor hues, and pulled it on as she hurried to get rid of whoever it was.

Scooping her hair back, she glanced through the peephole.

Her stomach did a quick dive into her bare toes even as her heart hit overdrive.

Livi took a deep breath, tightened the tie on her robe, then pulled open the door.

Oh, my.

He looked good.

He'd shaved—his jaw so smooth she wanted to glide her fingers over it. He wore slacks, an open-collar shirt that hovered between deep purple and black and a leather jacket that did justice to his broad shoulders.

Oh, yes. He looked very, *very* good.

"Hi," she finally remembered to say. "I didn't expect you so soon."

He was giving her the same inspection she'd given him, reminding Livi that she wasn't wearing a whole lot to inspect.

It took a few moments before Mitch pulled his gaze from her body, but eventually he looked up.

"I spend a lot of my life on a ship or sub, so showering fast is a habit," he told her, humor glinting in his eyes. "I did stop for these."

He handed Livi a bouquet.

"Peonies," she said softly, burying her face in the vivid pink blooms. "Thank you."

Then, realizing he was still standing in the hall, she stepped aside and gestured. "Please, come in. I'm sorry, I'm not quite ready yet."

"Is it a problem? Me being here," he asked, repeating her earlier question.

"Definitely not," she breathed. "Please, come in and be comfortable. It'll just take me a minute to be ready, but I want to put these in water first."

She hurried through the living room into the kitchen so she could put the flowers in water. She pulled an etched purple vase from the cabinet and added water and the flowers. She took a second to skim her fingers over the fragrant blooms and sigh, her eyes misting at his sweetness.

Deep breath. Get it together, she warned herself. *Don't want him to think you're a lovesick goofball.*

Vase in hand, she turned.

And almost busted it against his cast-iron belly.

"Oh, my God, I'm so sorry." Her words flew out in a rush of air, her pulse jumping in shock. Hands trapped between the glass and his abs, Livi barely bit back a groan. There she was, skipping the lovesick part and just proving that she was a goofball.

"I like your place," Mitch said as if she hadn't slammed him in the belly with his lovely gift. His smile calmed her in a way that no amount of reassuring words or deep breathing could do.

Suddenly Livi wasn't worried about how he thought of her. Because she could see it in his eyes. The admiration, the amused enjoyment. The desire.

Oh, my, there was a lot of desire in those blue depths.

Nervous again, but for totally different reasons now that the edgy needs were pulling at her, Livi turned and carefully set the vase in the center of the counter.

"I could show you around," she offered brightly as she turned back to Mitch. "As you can probably tell by the size of the kitchen, I'm not much of a chef."

"I've seen some pretty amazing things come out of small kitchens." Mitch slid a finger along her hair as it curved over her cheek. His words were innocent enough, especially given his earlier reminder that he spent so much time on ships. But his flirtatious tone and the heat in his gaze made it clear he wouldn't mind making her come in or out of the kitchen.

Livi's thighs turned to jelly, hot sticky awareness pooling between them at his words, at the look in his eyes. Her nipples beaded so tightly she was surprised they didn't burst through the silk of her bra. This was crazy. He had barely touched her and she was ready to explode.

Not sure how to handle the situation, Mitch or her own unfamiliar needs, Livi gave him a shaky smile before skirting around him and hurrying back into the living room.

As always, the soothing colors and soft lines calmed her. Then Mitch walked in and all she could wonder was how he'd look lying naked on her plush white carpet.

"Great lights," he said, indicating the strands of blue, purple and teal bulbs she'd draped around the French doors leading to the small balcony. "They match your furniture. Do you change them out for Christmas?"

Change them? Livi frowned at the lights. Why would she do that?

"I don't really decorate," she said instead. "It's just me, and I spend the actual holiday at my mom's…"

She gave an awkward shrug.

"So where did you want to go?" she asked, ready to change the subject.

His eyes locked on her, his expression that of an amused cat enjoying himself, Mitch stepped down into the sunken living room.

"Do you like Mexican food?" He moved closer, within touching distance, so Livi would only have to reach out her hand if she wanted to explore that gorgeous chest.

And oh, how she wanted to.

"I love Mexican food." She took a few steps backward, stopping when her calves hit the coffee table.

"Pedro's?" His smile heading toward wicked, Mitch took another step closer.

Her white dress would be perfect. Of course, with that look in Mitch's eyes, she was feeling pretty good in her robe, too.

"Pedro's is my favorite." She sidestepped along the edge of the table until she cleared it. But she didn't step back again. She didn't want him to think she was a chicken. "I have to go change. It won't take me a minute."

There was nothing chicken about that, she decided. And if she took a few minutes for a little pep talk and maybe to stick her head between her knees so she stopped hyperventilating, well, he wouldn't know.

"That's not what you're wearing?" Mitch teased as he

reached out to rub the fabric of her collar between two fingers. "It looks perfect to me."

His simple words were offered with a smile. But there was a look in his eyes that fascinated Livi. A promise of delights she'd never imagined, a solid confidence that he'd be the best she'd ever encounter.

Livi didn't know where it came from. She was never forward with men. Even after a year of marriage she'd always waited for Derrick to initiate sex.

But this was Mitch.

She felt things with him that she'd never felt before.

Edgy desire and white-hot need.

Tempting passion and naughty hunger.

And comfort.

As if she were safe. Not just physically safe because he was a SEAL. But safe to be herself, without fear of judgment or reprisal.

It was a total turn-on.

"Actually," she told him as she unknotted her robe, "I thought I might wear this."

It only took a tiny shrug to send the fabric sliding over her skin, down her body and to the floor.

Leaving her wearing two tiny bits of black silk and the heat of Mitch's gaze. Her nerves were gone. There was no room for them in a body filled with desire.

"You wear that and we're going to have some problems," Mitch said, his voice a little huskier than before. The hand that'd tested the fabric of her robe slid along her bare arm now, close enough to warm her breast but not touch it.

Craving coiled, low and tight in Livi's belly.

"What sort of problems?" she asked, not moving. Barely breathing.

"Hunger problems," he told her as his hand skimmed her waist now, up to the edge of her bra, then down her side to the tiny strip of lace at her hip. "We're definitely going to go hungry."

She didn't see him move.

She had no idea how he went from standing a foot away to sweeping her into his arms, but there she was. Livi gasped, wrapping her arms around his shoulders so she wouldn't fall. Then she realized she was in no danger of falling. At least, not onto the ground.

"Nobody's ever swept me off my feet before," she said, a little stunned.

"Let's see what else we can do that you've never done before," Mitch suggested just before his mouth took hers.

So many things were on her haven't-done-before list. But Livi was pretty sure she'd be crossing a few off tonight.

And then she stopped thinking and just felt.

Because his lips were magic.

They brushed over hers, and Livi's body trembled.

They pressed tighter, his tongue teasing its way into her mouth, and Livi's heart raced.

They slid, angled, seduced. And Livi melted.

Her fingers skimmed the short, soft hair at his nape while the other hand explored the delicious breadth of his shoulder. The man was an ode to physical perfection. She couldn't wait to see more, to touch more. Was he that hard everywhere?

Heat wound tighter in her belly, her thighs pressed together to intensify the trembling need dampening her panties, making her quiver.

His kiss deepened, his tongue sliding along hers in a swirling, seductive dance. Livi swore she felt herself falling, the sensations were so amazing. It was like floating on a silken cloud of delight.

Mitch's hands skimmed down her waist to grasp her hips, his thumbs teasing her pelvic bones before they smoothed their way back up her torso to cup her breasts.

Livi's eyes flew open as a tiny explosion burst through her, starting at her clitoris and fanning out in a swirling wave of pleasure.

"How…" Her breathless question trailed away unasked when she realized she was laying sideways across her bed, Mitch standing above staring down at her.

Echoes of her climax breezed through her, gentle and sweet, relaxing her muscles, warming her body for the next round.

"How…?" he prompted, his blue eyes intensely focused on his fingers as they cupped her breasts, molding the aching flesh through her silk bra.

"Um, how did you find my bedroom?" she improvised. It sounded better than *"How did you sprout two extra arms and make me come while still carrying me?"*

"I'm good at finding things," he told her with that slow smile of his. "Now why don't I find a few other things you might like?"

"I'll bet I can find a few you'll like, too," Livi offered, using her abdominals to pull herself into a sitting position so her mouth was level with his belly. Or, if she leaned down a little, her lips would be in touching distance of that very, *very* impressive erection straining the zipper of his slacks.

Before she could decide where to start, Mitch gripped her shoulders. When Livi glanced up, he shook his head.

"This time, this first time, let's do it my way," he suggested in a seductively low tone.

Livi wet her lips, nerves dancing in time with the images flashing through her imagination. Nerves, and excitement.

"What, exactly, is *your way*?" she asked.

Mitch reached down to slide the smooth strap of her bra down the curve of her shoulder, loosening the silk cup and relieving a little of the pressure on her right breast. Then he did the same with the left strap. The wispy fabric draped low, catching on Livi's turgid nipples. The sensation of the silk tugging ever so lightly sent a shaft of pleasure through her.

"My way is to strip you bare," Mitch said, tracing the tips of his fingers over the full curve of one breast, then the other. "I want to see your body spread over this bed, to watch you as I touch every inch. To hear your excitement when I kiss my way over every erogenous zone you have."

Livi shivered with need.

"And what am I doing as you have your way?" she asked, barely getting the words out because her throat was so dry.

Mitch leaned forward, close enough for Livi to press her cheek against his hip bone. Her hands gripped his butt—what an amazing ass he had—and squeezed as she tried to scoot even closer. But he moved away before she could. His hands grasped her wrists, gently moving her arms back to her sides.

"My way means I'm going to worship your body," he told her quietly. "While I have my way, there's only one thing I want you to do."

Livi found herself nodding before he even told her what it was. She didn't care. She'd do anything to continue feeling this good, to feel even better. She started to lift one hand to grab him again but found her hand trapped. Glancing down, she saw her wrists bracketed by her bra straps and realized he'd unhooked it when he'd leaned forward.

She frowned at the black silk, trying to move her hands again. Had he knotted it? Her hands were at least six inches apart, but they were definitely tied together.

Her startled eyes flew back to Mitch's face, noting his wicked smile.

"What do you want me to do?" she finally asked when she realized he'd stand there waiting until she did.

"Lay back and enjoy."

That's it?

It sounded so simple.

But it wasn't.

It wasn't just that Livi had spent the last year of her marriage doing most of the sexual heavy lifting—so to speak—in an attempt to make it up to Derrick that she couldn't get pregnant. It was that for all their apparent desperation to get their hands on her body, she'd never had a man actually worship her.

It should be easy to lay back and let him give her pleasure.

But that required trust.

So, so many levels of trust.

She surreptitiously tried to free her hands, but the slippery fabric wouldn't budge. Before she could decide if she was worried or not, Mitch began unbuttoning his shirt.

Livi's breath caught in her chest, her eyes eating him up inch by inch as the dark fabric parted. He tugged the shirt from his waistband, releasing the last few buttons. She wet her lips then sucked the bottom one between her teeth and waited.

He shrugged off his shirt.

She moaned quietly.

He was gorgeous. Despite the calendar saying December, Mitch's body was a golden tan, the sprinkling of black hair on his chest emphasizing perfectly sculpted pectorals. His waist tapered, angling down to frame a six-pack that made her thirsty for everything he had to offer.

He kicked off his shoes, and Livi hummed.

But then he stopped.

Frowning, she gave him a saucy look.

"More?"

"Lay back."

Livi glanced at the bed before focusing on Mitch's pants. His erection was impressive behind that straining zipper, but she wanted to see it free, to touch it, feel it, taste it.

"But—"

Mitch hooked one finger through the fabric of her bra where it rested in her lap. His knuckle rubbed against her panties, right above her mound. Her clitoris quivered, needy, wet and aching.

Livi laid back. Her knees bent and her feet on the floor, she left her hands on her belly until Mitch gave them a questioning look.

Livi's heart pounded, her pulse racing as if she'd run a four-minute mile. She swallowed hard. Trying not to squirm at the wet heat pooling between her thighs, she slowly raised her hands overhead, resting them on her hair where it pillowed around her like a halo. It wouldn't have been an unfamiliar position if she were doing crunches, but she'd never had to be in it almost naked.

From Mitch's smile, he knew that. And he liked it.

Then his gaze shifted to her body. His expression changed, amusement fading into desire. His fingers trailed over her knees, which automatically moved aside so he could step between them. He pressed his palms against her thighs, sliding them upward so they caught on the fabric of her panties.

Was he going to pull them off? Rip them away? Livi's breath hitched and she tried not to squirm, even though she wanted to. More, she wanted to shift, to press herself against one of those hands and force him to ease some of the building pressure.

He angled his fingers to skim along the elastic at her thighs from the sides inward. Closer and closer. She shifted her hips higher, needing him to touch her, wanting to know what he could do, how he'd make her feel.

But before he got to her core, he slid his fingers back and pressed his palms flat again.

"Tease," she breathed, her word a puff of air.

"I'll make you a deal," he promised, giving her a wink

as his hands caressed the flat planes of her stomach. "For every bit of teasing I do, you're welcome to do your own. Later."

Oh, now that was a deal Livi would enjoy. Her smile bloomed, but before she could tell him what she'd do, his hands cupped her breasts. He caught her nipples between two fingers, holding and pinching at the same time.

Livi's hips bucked, her body hot and tight, right there on orgasm's sweet edge. He continued gently squeezing her full breasts, her nipples rolling between his knuckles. Her breath came so fast, her throat was on fire. She leaned her head back, closing her eyes and reveling in the feel of his incredible hands.

She felt him move closer, bare skin sliding along her inner thighs. *Oh, please, yes*, her body begged. She wanted him so badly, needed him inside her.

Her eyes flew open when wet heat swirled around her nipple. His stiff tongue circled, teased, flicked, even as his hands still kneaded her so that she felt each rhythmic squeeze deep in her abdomen.

"You like that?" he asked, watching her as he licked.

"Oh, my, yes," she breathed, arching her back.

He released one breast, shifting her hands so they were cupped behind her head, angling her neck so she could watch. Livi had never watched a man pleasure her before, but she obeyed Mitch's silent demand.

His eyes locked on hers as he sucked the aching, hard nipple into his mouth. She gasped, feeling rather than seeing him work it between his teeth even as his tongue soothed her.

Her hips undulated, trying to find the right pressure, the right angle, to relieve some of the building tension.

But his chest was pressed against her belly, so she couldn't find relief. Instead, the need coiled more and more tightly.

He ran his tongue over her breast, swirling a wet path up the other one, sucking the nipple in his mouth. At the same time, his fingers pinched the wet flesh he'd just left. Livi didn't think she'd ever felt anything as incredible, had ever had anyone so intimately aware of her body as Mitch was now.

As if he heard her thought and just had to show her how much more intimate he'd be getting, his fingers slipped under her panties, pulling the fabric aside. Cool air hit hot flesh, the contrast its own turn-on. Then Mitch pinched her wet, aching bud between his fingers, sliding, teasing, tormenting.

Livi curved her back, needing more.

"You like this?"

She couldn't even find the breath to say yes. All she could do was moan. A long, throaty agreement because, oh, that felt good.

He must have liked her answer, because he slid down her body to angle himself between her thighs. She didn't feel the fabric tear, didn't know if he'd pulled her panties off or they'd simply melted in her heat, but suddenly, his mouth was there.

His tongue touched her bud and slid along its wet length. With that one touch, all of Livi's thoughts disappeared. Sensation took over. Hot, vivid sensation filled with an edgy sort of need.

He lifted her thighs so they draped over his shoulders, then shifted himself higher, so her hips were off the bed. His eyes locked on hers. All Livi could see was a brilliant blue as she watched him sip at her.

Then his fingers were on her nipples again, plucking, thrumming, playing her. His tongue speared into her core, the throbbing inner walls gripping him as tiny spirals of pleasure burst, collided and expanded into a mind-blowing orgasm.

As she exploded into a million pieces of pleasure, her eyes stayed open, stayed on his. The look on his face sent her even higher, called up yet another climax, this one so powerful her entire body shook.

Everything went black. She could hear her cries, could feel his mouth, pressed herself tighter against his fingers. And she went over a third time, only one thought working through the sensations racking her body.

Super Hottie, indeed.

GOD, SHE WAS AMAZING.

Mitch sipped, delighting in Livi's ambrosia as he watched her explode.

He had a firm handle on his body, knew how to use its responses, how to delay its reactions. In part that was training, but mostly it was innate. He liked control.

But his control was being seriously tested right now. Livi's cries beckoned, tempting him to the edge. The sight of her body, so lush yet muscled, so gorgeously responsive, had him hard and ready to burst.

But it was the feel of her that was seducing him brainless.

She was silk over steel, soft golden skin stretched over well-developed muscles. He'd never realized how erotic a strong woman was. From her full breasts to her flat abs to the corded length of her calves, every inch of her was making him crazy.

He wanted to touch it all. He needed to taste it all.

But with every slide of his hand, every shift of her body, he came closer and closer to that edge.

He reveled in the way her thighs gripped his arms, his torso, and strained toward his dick as he slowly lowered her to the bed.

Mitch unhooked his slacks, his hand on the zipper when Livi gave a low moan, stretching her arms overhead and twisting her body in a writhing sort of undulation. Her lashes fluttered open, those pretty brown eyes dazed as she stared up at him.

Then she smiled.

A slow, sensual smile, and wet her lips.

"Mm," she murmured, raising one knee and trailing her own fingers along her thigh, across her stomach, over one full, pouting breast and to her lips. Her smile mischievous, she pressed a kiss to those fingers and blew it his way. "Want a real one?"

More than he wanted his next breath.

"Then c'mon. Do me now, Super Hottie," she invited.

Mitch swore he heard the snap as his control broke. He ripped off his pants, barely remembering to grab a condom from the pocket before he dove onto the bed.

Livi's delighted laugh quickly turned to cries of pleasure as his hands raced over her body. Squeezing, tweaking, teasing. He took her mouth, needing to taste her.

His tongue thrust in and out, slowly at first, then faster and faster to foreshadow what was about to come. Livi's fingers dug into his shoulders, her pelvis arching, begging.

His body was on fire. She slipped a hand free from her restraints and swept down, nails scraping gently over his abs, fingers wrapping like a velvet vice around his throbbing dick. He almost came right then and there. Had to grab fast to the edge of the cliff before he flew right over. Not yet, he chanted silently. Not without her.

He angled his body out of her reach. She gave a keening moan of protest, the sound turning into a gasp when he took her nipple between his teeth.

Testing, his fingers dipped, swirled.

Her breath shortened. He felt her body tense, knew she was close. His fingers still working her, he sipped at her breast while sheathing himself with his free hand.

Livi's moans grew short.

Her fingers scrambled over his body, scraping, kneading.

He drew back a little, breathing a hot puff of air on her wet nipple.

She exploded.

He couldn't look away. She was incredible to watch. Color painted her cheeks, poured over her breasts. Her back arched as she milked every ounce of pleasure out of her climax.

So what else could Mitch do but make sure she had another one? Before the last wave ebbed, he plunged in.

He wanted to feel that pleasure, needed to be inside her while she came.

She was so tight. So strong.

Her thighs clamped onto his hips, her abs tight and hard as she dug her heels into the bed, her body angled to meet his thrusts. The harder he plunged, the faster and louder she moaned.

She was so responsive.

So perfect.

Perfect for him.

Even as that thought terrified him, it sent a piercing shaft of pleasure though him like a bolt of lightning. Mitch gave over to his body, letting it take control.

Pleasure built, layered, tightened. His focus narrowed to a pinpoint. All he could see was Livi's face.

All he could feel was need as she continued to meet his thrusts, adding a little undulation on each one. The twisting friction pushed his final button.

Mitch plunged once.

Twice.

He paused and tried to hold back the pounding waves of pleasure, but he couldn't.

He plunged again.

And exploded.

Over and over and over, he rode the explosion. Colors

flashing, his body trembling. Through it all, he felt Livi's hands, so soft as they soothed his body, rubbed his back. Made his return as much a pleasure as his blastoff.

As he slowly drifted back to awareness, Mitch rolled onto his side, wrapping Livi tight in his arms as he did. Her body trembled, gratifying proof that she still felt the power of their lovemaking.

She blew his mind.

Mitch had never been a selfish man—especially not in bed. He considered it as much a pleasure to send his partner over the edge as he did to go over himself.

He'd never felt like this before.

He didn't know if that was a good thing or a bad thing.

But it was definitely a real thing.

His hands cupped her butt, pulling her closer. Mitch buried his face in Livi's hair.

Everything about her appealed to him.

Everything about her fascinated him.

This was so, so real.

8

"THIS IS DELICIOUS. How do you eat like *this* and still have a body like *that*?"

Livi laughed as she swirled angel hair pasta around her fork, the rich scent of tomato, basil and garlic filling the air.

"It's not a very high-calorie meal," she said with a shrug. Just dried pasta, a quick homemade sauce and wine-sautéed chicken breasts. Derrick hadn't liked it, saying it wasn't spaghetti if it didn't have meatballs—not surprising from a man with a ball fetish. "I tend to stick with fresh ingredients and simple preparations. Nothing fancy. Besides, I exercise for a living, remember?"

He gave her a long look, his blue eyes traveling over her body like a hot caress. Dressed in flannel sleep shorts and a thin tank top that showed as much as it concealed, her hair bundled up in a messy ponytail and her feet bare, Livi knew she wasn't at her best. But that expression in his eyes made her feel as if she was perfect.

"Your body is a credit to your career," he said as he toasted her with his fork. "And this meal a credit to great flavor."

"I'm glad you like it." Livi smiled, pleasure wrapping through her at his praise.

"It's great. Fresh, healthy, delicious." As if to prove his point, Mitch ate his last bite and eyed hers. Still on her first serving, which was a quarter of either of his, Livi leaned forward to scoop half of her chicken and what was left of her own pasta onto his empty plate. As she settled back into her cozy spot on the floor, she rested her elbows on the glass coffee table, her chin on her knuckles and her heart on her sleeve.

What a night.

Had she ever been made love to like that? It took all of a millisecond to review her history and come up with a resounding "never." The first time had blown her mind. The second had been a surprise—apparently Super Hotties didn't need much downtime between rounds of pleasure—that'd quickly turned to delight when Mitch gave her the same free rein with his body as he'd demanded of hers the first round.

Livi had collapsed on top of him after that one, falling into a deep, dreamless sleep.

They'd opted to eat in the living room instead of on stools at the kitchen counter. For ambiance, she'd turned on her version of Christmas lights—a string of blue, green and purple bulbs draped along the ceiling. Mitch was spread out comfortably across her couch, but Livi had chosen to sit cross-legged on the floor across from him to enjoy the view.

And what a view he was.

Unselfconsciously naked but for his navy-blue boxers, he didn't appear to have an ounce of spare body fat. Instead, he was pure, gorgeous muscled perfection.

And he knew it.

No wonder the man oozed self-confidence. He obviously didn't let anyone push him around. Probably because nobody had the strength.

It wasn't a physical thing.

She had muscles, and without being conceited, she knew she had a rockin' body. That was her job.

The confidence to stand up, to keep anyone from pushing her around? That didn't come from healthy eating and strength training. She wished it did.

Of course, that wish came with the question…

What would she do if she had that sort of confidence?

Who would she face down?

What would she change?

Wanting was so easy.

But going for it?

That was another story.

Then again…

Her eyes trailed over Mitch's body, her mouth going dry.

She'd wanted Mitch. Probably more than she could remember wanting anything or anyone else in her life.

And she'd had him.

Oh, my, she'd had him in so many delicious ways.

But had she gone for him? Was it enough that she'd gone along for the ride, if she ended up exactly where she wanted?

It could be.

But that was the easy way.

She watched the play of muscles as Mitch lifted his fork, his bicep rippling effortlessly, his abs tightening when he twisted to set his plate on the table. Her eyes dropped to the only part of his body not showing skin. She'd never wished for a tighty-whitey kind of guy, but she'd bet they'd offer a better view right now.

She wanted to see him naked.

Wanted to feast her eyes on every single one of his muscles. To stroke, pet, lick them. She wanted to watch him grow, to see if she could inspire him to new lengths. Long, hard new lengths.

She let out a shaky breath.

Maybe hard was a whole lot better than easy.

She gave a little shiver.

"You cold?"

Livi blinked, then mentally replayed the question.

Cold?

Oh, my, no.

"Just hungry," she told him quietly.

"Oops." Mitch shot a rueful glance at his clean plate.

But she wasn't hungry for food.

Livi was pretty sure if she waited, Mitch would feed that hunger without any prompting from her. He'd probably come up with an even better way to do it, too. Something creatively sexy, like he'd done when he'd tied her wrists together. She shivered at the memory, delighting in the idea of waiting, in letting him take control.

But there was something about Mitch that made her want to prove herself. Livi wanted him to see her as an equal. As a source of as much pleasure and excitement as she saw him.

Even more, she wanted him to feel the helpless need for her, that intense craving that she had for him. There were so many levels of need. She didn't just want him to need her body in a way that any woman could fill.

She wanted him to need her to answer the desires she, and she alone, inspired. The ones she stirred up through her actions, through her imagination and through her demands on him.

"Want dessert? I thought I saw strawberries in the fridge."

"Strawberries are nice," Livi replied in the same quiet, contemplative tone as before.

As she said it, she realized nice would never stick with a man like Mitch. Nice was okay, but forgettable. Nice could be replaced with good or okay or not bad.

Livi wet her lips and slowly got to her feet.

She would never forget Mitch.

She didn't want him to ever forget her, either.

Which meant she had to go for it and get beyond "nice."

Her eyes locked on his, she moved around the coffee table to stand beside him. A part of her, the one that always wanted to hide instead of talk to people, whispered for her to take the plate and pretend she was simply tidying up.

Livi took a deep breath and hushed that whisper.

Instead, she crossed her arms over her stomach, grabbed the hem of her tank and pulled it overhead.

His brows shot up.

What was the worst he could do?

Say, "No, thank you." I don't want my body worshipped right now.

Determined, she leaned forward and hooked her fingers in the elastic band of his shorts, then tugged.

"You're not going to find strawberries in there," he said with a husky laugh. But he didn't stop her. Instead, he angled his hips so she could slide the fabric off.

"I'm not hungry for strawberries."

"What are you hungry for?"

Even his words pushed her, challenging her to say aloud what she wanted. She glanced at the smooth length of his already hardening erection and skimmed her finger around the satiny head.

"I'm hungry for a different kind of dessert," she told him with a wicked smile, straddling his long, hard body, delighting in the feel of him between her thighs.

"Is that a fact?" he asked, his voice even huskier.

"Oh, yeah."

Livi shimmied down his chest, over his hips until she straddled his thighs, making sure to slide the pebbled tips of her breasts over his flesh as she went.

"Livi…"

Before he could finish his sentence, she took him into her mouth. And oh, my, what a mouthful he was.

Livi lost herself in his taste, sliding her tongue along the thick fullness of his cock. He was so big, so hard. So yummy.

"Livi…"

She sucked on the head as if she could draw his essence into her, as if she could absorb and share some of his power.

His fingers tunneled into her hair, tangling in the pony-tail, gripping her scalp.

She didn't know if he was trying to hold her closer or pull her farther away. She didn't care. Her teeth scraped along his length.

He hissed, arching his hips.

She blew a puff of cool air on his wet flesh.

His free hand fisted into the couch cushion.

She slid her mouth up, then down. Sucking and sipping.

"Livi."

This time he didn't trail off, didn't lose track.

Instead he jackknifed himself into a sitting position, grabbed her by the waist and flipped her around so she was still straddling him, but facing his feet. She heard the fabric of her sleep shorts rip before she felt the cool air on her hot core. Before she felt the even hotter spear of his tongue sliding over her swollen flesh.

Her hair falling over her face and shoulders now, she let it blanket her as she leaned down to once again delight in her new favorite dessert, Mitch's engorged erection.

Heat swirled, tension built with every flick of his tongue. Livi wanted to fly over, needed the satisfaction that his fingers promised as they teased and tempted.

But not until he came first.

Determined, feeling as if her every hope of keeping Mitch's attention after this one orgasm rested on who came first, she ran the edge of her teeth gently around the head, her hand sliding along the shaft in the same rhythm in which his tongue worked her.

She felt him tense.

He grabbed her hip with one hand, as if to warn her to slow down.

So Livi sped up.

She felt his juices rising, felt his body preparing to explode. Triumph surged, adding its own layer of pleasure to the delight his tongue was offering.

"Livi, now," he growled against her clitoris.

"Make me," she challenged right back.

"Damn it."

She would have laughed with triumph, but her mouth was full.

Then it wasn't.

Livi gave a startled cry as Mitch moved her so fast the room blurred. One second she was straddling his body, ready to take him into heaven.

The next she was belly-down on the couch, his body poised behind her, seeking entry.

Livi angled up and welcomed him in.

The second he hit her wet heat, he lost it.

His explosion sent her flying, her body shattering into a million pieces. And each one of those pieces was filled with satisfaction and delight.

"How do you do it?"

Her lush body curled naked in his arms, her fingers tracing random patterns on his chest. Mitch didn't figure Livi was referring to his holding her upright against the shower wall while he'd poured himself into her welcoming body.

But since that was the last thing he remembered before dropping into bed with her, he wasn't sure what she did mean.

"Do what?"

"All of it." She propped herself up on her elbows, giving him a superb view of her breasts through the tangled blonde curls falling over her shoulder. "I mean, it can't be easy to juggle everything, to handle all the responsibilities and challenges in your career."

Her words trailed off as Livi bit her lip and looked away

for a moment. Was she trying to figure out how to ask him about that career?

His body, so wonderfully relaxed just a moment ago, tensed in anticipation.

What he did was classified. From the code he used, to the places he went, to the targets he engaged, every real aspect of his career was top secret. Which meant he didn't talk about it, except with his fellow teammates, and then only if they were serving on the same mission. Hell, he didn't discuss ninety-five percent of what he did with his father or grandfather, and they were both active duty superior officers.

And this was why he usually kept his liaisons short and sweet, he thought with a sigh. Livi was different. He wouldn't tell her anything, but for now while she was naked and vulnerable, he'd sidestep lightly. Then later, he'd make sure she understood the parameters.

"It's my job. I chose it. I train for it. I do it. That's all there really is to say." He kept his tone light and easy but steeled himself for her reaction.

"That's what I mean," she said, putting her weight on one elbow so she could gesture with her other hand. The move did intriguing things to his view, but not enough to ease Mitch's tension. "How do you do that? You're amazing. You do the impossible and simply accept that it's doable. You must face insurmountable odds, but you have such an even temperament. Then there's everything you must have faced. But you still smile. Is it innate? Were you born with that confidence or is it something you've built over time, layer by successful layer?"

When he could only stare, shocked to his core, Livi's shoulders drooped a little. She wrinkled her nose then shrugged, as if dismissing her own question.

"I suppose it's a crazy question. I guess I'm just…" She hesitated. "I'm fascinated by what makes people strong.

Probably a quirk of the job I do, I guess. I'm always interested in building layers of strength. You're one of the stron-
gest, most self-assured people I've ever met."

That wasn't what she'd been about to say, but he let it go.
Mostly because he was stunned by her words.

"You humble me," he said quietly. "And you make me
sound much more—much bigger—than I am."

This time Livi's head shake was emphatic, her brow fur-
rowed in a stubborn frown.

"Oh, no. You're definitely all that. When I first saw you
at Roz's, I called you Super Hottie in my head," she told
him with a shy sort of laugh. "But it's not a joke. You really are a superhero. You're the leading man who saves the
world. I don't think it's because you're a SEAL, although
I'm sure that adds to it. I think it's simply who you are.
Strong, confident, sure."

"You're mixing up personality with my training," he
decided. "I'm one of the best because that's what being a
SEAL means. That's what we're trained for."

"If you weren't a SEAL, you'd still be one of the best,"
she argued. "I'll bet you were the best all through school.
I'd wager you excel in whatever you do when you're not
being a SEAL, too."

Well, yeah. Of course he did. Why wouldn't he?

Watching Livi's fingers comb through the silky length
of her hair, Mitch frowned.

His entire life he'd been given compliments, accolades,
approval. He'd never questioned his right to those things,
just as he'd never deliberately sought them out. They were
simply a part of his world.

He was one of the best.

That wasn't ego.

It was simply fact.

Because he expected it to be. Because everyone else in

his life expected it, as well. Mitch didn't think he'd ever considered another option.

But neither had he ever considered it special, something to be admired to the degree that Livi seemed to think it deserved. He'd have chalked it up to great sex combined with a little hero worship, but that's not what he saw in her eyes.

He wasn't sure exactly what it was that he saw in those blue depths, though.

Confused, a little blown away, Mitch couldn't find the words to tell her how she made him feel.

So he showed her instead.

He pulled her into his arms, keeping his kisses gentle, his touch tender.

He wanted to show her how incredible *she* was, not talk about how special she thought he was.

He felt her instant flare of passion but worked to bank it. He wanted her to simmer, not boil over.

He wanted her to float on desire, not catapult into passion.

He simply wanted her.

With a gentleness and care he'd never realized he had, Mitch worshiped Livi.

Worshipped her body.

Her spirit.

Her beautiful sweetness.

As he did, he felt something shift.

But he felt too good to worry about it.

He sent her up in a smooth, easy wave. Then he followed, sliding home and letting himself ride that wave as her cries washed over them both.

Incredible.

She made him feel so good.

Her body blanketed over his, he felt Livi drift off to sleep against him. It was only then that Mitch himself relaxed.

His head was spinning. His emotions, too, although they were revolving in the opposite direction. The combination was overwhelming and just a little nauseating. Like a carnival ride gone haywire.

Mitch spent a considerable portion of his time in danger, risking life and limb, facing impossible odds to bring down extreme enemies. He was a skillfully trained, highly specialized expert who lived on the edge.

So he made it a point to balance the rest of his life against that.

He'd basically excelled in most of his pursuits.

He'd surrounded himself with people who inspired him, with challenges he enjoyed.

And he'd always considered his sex life to be strong and healthy. He'd never wanted for more than he had.

Until he'd met Livi.

Now, he couldn't imagine sex without her.

He was a little worried that he couldn't even imagine his life without her.

He wanted to write that thought off to exhaustion and maybe a little sexual haze. But he knew better.

Like everything in his life—simple or complicated—Mitch faced it head-on. He had feelings for the woman in his arms. He didn't know what they were yet, but he'd have to figure it out. Soon.

And when he did, it'd be fine.

Whatever it was.

Mitch had never faced anything, anyone, any situation, that he couldn't figure out and make work in his favor. It might not work immediately, but it always worked eventually.

Whatever this was with Livi would be no different.

So for now, he'd simply enjoy it. With that last thought, Mitch tucked his chin into Livi's sweetly scented hair and drifted into a deep, dreamless sleep.

WHO KNEW THE area around her apartment building was so quiet at three in the morning? Then again, she'd never stood on her balcony in the wee hours, watching the moonlight glint off the ocean.

"It's almost hypnotic," she murmured.

"A seductress," Mitch agreed, his arm warm around her shoulder and his body heating the right side of hers. "She's had me hooked as long as I can remember."

"Is that why you joined the Navy? Because you love the ocean?" Was that why her father had left her and her mother? Because he couldn't resist the call of the waves?

"The Navy is a family tradition," Mitch said, his voice pitched low, in keeping with the cool night. "I'd have joined regardless. But yeah, I do love the ocean."

"Is it different where you're from? You live in Virginia most of the time, don't you?" Just saying the words hurt, like a fist-to-the-gut reminder that he was temporary. But she'd known that, she chided herself. She'd gone into this relationship with her eyes wide open. Besides, everything was temporary. Her marriage had taught her that.

Still, she shifted a little more tightly against Mitch's body, as if she could hold on to the feel of him for just a little longer.

"I was last stationed in Virginia," he said in such an agreeable tone that Livi wondered what that was double-speak for. "But I've sailed on every ocean. None of them is the same, not as another, not from day to day."

Watching the silvery glint of moonlight on the far-off waves, Livi cuddled in his arms as Mitch described the Atlantic in the winter, the Indian Ocean in the summer. He spoke of places she'd never heard of and a few she'd always dreamed of seeing.

There was so much passion in his voice. The same sort she used to have for fitness, she realized. But more, there was a reverence, layered with quiet assurance. He respected the ocean's power and was humbled by its magnificence. He knew he belonged there. He was a part of that magnificent power.

She was in awe.

And she realized, as he talked about an ice storm in the Arctic, she was freezing.

Despite the blanket she'd wrapped around her before they'd come out, and the warmth of Mitch's body, Livi shivered. Her cheeks felt like ice and her poor toes were shaking against the tiles beneath them.

"You're cold," Mitch noted. "We should go in."

"No," she protested quickly. "I don't want to go in yet."

She'd never had a romantic moment like this before. She didn't want it to end. Not yet.

"At least let me go inside and get your coat."

"I don't have one. Maybe I just need to put some socks on."

"You don't have a coat?"

He sounded so shocked she had to laugh.

"What can I say?" she told him with a shrug. "I grew up in southern California. I don't need much in the way of winter clothes."

"You must at least have some sort of winter wear."

"Jackets, sure." She shrugged. Noticing that he was looking at her like she'd grown an extra head, she thought fast. "I do have a ski parka." She waited a beat before honesty forced her to admit, "But it's in storage with my ski equipment."

Solving the problem, Mitch pulled her around so her back faced his front, wrapped his arms tight around her waist and shifted her upward. Her feet were off the tiles, her body suspended against his. She wasn't sure what super SEAL power he'd called on, but she suddenly felt as if her entire body was filled with heat.

Maybe it was lust. She hoped so. Because it was starting to feel scarily close to some other L word.

"You ski?"

"Sure. It's a great workout, and always makes me feel better about having extra whipped cream on my post-ski hot chocolate. There's this little lodge in Vail that adds homemade peppermint sprinkles to theirs at Christmas. I almost went back this year just for that treat alone."

"Does your family join you to celebrate when you travel?"

Join her? Livi almost asked why, but she stopped herself. He didn't need to know how dysfunctional her meager family was.

"I went with friends last year," she said instead. Then, shivering from something other than cold, she added, "It's hard to believe it's almost Christmas."

"And we're standing outside in bare feet," Mitch said with a quiet laugh, taking the hint she hadn't realized she'd tossed out. "Let's go inside. You can make hot chocolate."

"You want hot chocolate?" she asked with a narrow look as they returned through the kitchen.

"Sure."

So she made hot chocolate.

"What's with the frown?" she asked, noting that the furrow between his brows had deepened as she heated milk and opened a bright red tin to add shaved chocolate into mugs. "Do you prefer a different kind?"

"I don't know yet." He took the mug she handed him, peered into it suspiciously and took a sip. He got the same look in his eyes as he'd had earlier when he'd watched her get naked. Excited, eager and very, very appreciative. This time his sip was closer to a gulp. "This is amazing."

"Oh, good." She sipped hers to test it, then added another sprinkle of chocolate shavings and stirred it. She lifted the tin in question, but Mitch moved his mug away as if protecting its contents. Livi giggled. "I'm sorry I don't have whipped cream or peppermint."

"This is perfect." He gestured for Livi to precede him and followed her into the living room. She curled up on the corner of her couch, her feet tucked under her and the blanket still wrapped tightly around her shoulders as he sat next to her. "I had no idea hot chocolate could taste like this."

He finished his and set the mug on the table, looking so wistful that Livi laughed and handed him what was left of hers.

"You sure?"

"Enjoy," she encouraged. She'd rather watch him, anyway.

"I always thought hot chocolate was brown powder in a pouch poured over water heated in the microwave," he told her. "That's how my mom always made it. She did add tiny marshmallows to it at the holidays, though."

"So hot chocolate is a holiday treat for both of us," she murmured, liking that connection.

"Speaking of." He made a show of looking around the room. "Christmas is only a few days away. When do you put the rest of your decorations up? Do you wait for Christmas Eve?"

Decorations?

For just her?

"The rest of them?" she asked, instead of admitting she didn't own any decorations. Derrick had taken the ones they'd bought together when he'd left as an extra "screw you" gesture, and she'd never bothered to replace them.

"You have lights up." With the now empty mug, he moved his hand toward the lights strung just below the crown molding around the room.

"Oh, those. They aren't exactly traditional holiday lights. They're blue and purple instead of red and green." Before he could comment, she said, "I'll bet you're a traditional guy all the way, right? Red and green lights, mistletoe and holly, carols and hot chocolate."

He stacked her drained mug under his on the table and shot her a grin.

"Don't forget my stellar rendition as a reindeer in the school play, my tromping through snow with my dad to cut down a tree and haul it home on my toboggan, or my searching for gifts before they were wrapped—the beginning of my stealth ops training."

"Did you ever get caught?" Livi asked eagerly, suddenly voracious to know anything and everything she could about him.

"I was never actually caught in the act," he said, his eyes dancing at what must be a delight of memories. "But it was funny. I always found something hidden away, though it never ended up under the tree. It took me four years to realize my parents must have left some sort of triggering device or tell, so they'd know if I found the gifts. I asked the old man about it once when I was at the academy. My mom did all the shopping, but he was in charge of hiding those gifts. He said he'd figured it was good practice in case I wanted to go into intelligence."

"Intelligence. That's like spy stuff, right? So did you want that?"

Mitch laughed and rested his arm on the back of the couch so he could play with her hair.

"Nothing that glamorous, and no. I always wanted to be a SEAL. The intelligence training, both early on and later from the Navy, is an asset, though. The old man takes credit for that."

Had her mother ever talked about her accomplishments like that? Livi didn't think so. Certainly not with the same loving pride she could see Mitch had gotten.

"It sounds as if you and your dad are close," she said, delighting in the image of him as a young boy. His parents clearly adored him. She wondered how much that unconditional acceptance played into that bone-deep confidence of his.

He shrugged, accepting that closeness, that unconditional love, as his due. What must that feel like?

"He's a great guy. My grandfather is an admiral, a real hard-ass." Mitch's smile was so affectionate Livi realized that must be a compliment. "That's a hard act to follow, but the old man didn't try. I asked about that once when I was a kid. I was trying to figure out how I was going to live up to their reputations."

"What did he say?" Livi leaned forward, fascinated. What kind of kid thought of those things?

"He told me he'd walked the same path but didn't walk in grandfather's footsteps. That I'd walk my own path, side by side, if I chose." Mitch shrugged, as if trying to shake off a little of the heavy emotion in his voice.

"Will you tell your own child that some day?" she wondered, a little part of her heart shying away from the difficult question. But she could imagine it so clearly, she wasn't able to resist asking.

"I doubt I'll have any. I'd want to be the kind of father my own was, but given my career, I don't see that happening." He gave a rueful laugh. "I guess that's part of my path, isn't it? Choosing not to go that route."

Despite the grief stabbing at her heart, Livi managed to smile.

Looked like she really had found the perfect guy.

9

LIVI HAD FORGOTTEN what morning looked like, given that she'd spent the last few in Mitch's arms, sleeping off sexually induced exhaustion.

Except this morning they'd both woken at six, too hungry to have more sex until they'd refueled. But when she'd suggested her usual, a bowl of Greek yogurt and fresh fruit, Mitch had looked at her as if she'd just asked him to wear her panties. Shocked, amused and a little horrified.

He'd handed her a glass of juice, settled her on a stool and taken over her kitchen. Until she'd started watching a bare-chested Mitch bustling around in her kitchen, whipping up pancake batter and chatting about the holidays, she'd had no clue how sexy cooking could be.

"You take hot breakfast to a whole 'nother level," Livi teased him when they sat down at the bistro table on her balcony. "It's enough to tempt a woman into wanting pancakes for two every day."

"A high compliment from a woman dedicated to breakfast for one," he said with a laugh.

"Why do you say that?" she asked, truly curious.

He frowned and handed her the bowl of fruit.

"Why else would you be single? A woman with your looks, personality, brains? It has to be by choice."

It did? Was that a bad thing? Before she could ask, Mitch continued.

"You know, as much as anyone ever had a choice."

Livi frowned at him.

"What do you mean?"

He shrugged.

"It's nice to believe we have a vast array of options in life, but in reality they are pretty limited. Gender, nationality, even family and upbringing, they all craft the bulk of our life choices." He stabbed at least half a dozen pancakes to transfer to his plate before handing her the platter. "It all factors in to the point that the vast majority of our life choices are predetermined."

Still holding the pancake platter aloft, Livi could only stare as she worked through that concept. Even after looking at it this way, then that, she still wasn't sure if she agreed or not.

She did know that Mitch baffled her.

They'd spent every moment of the last week together, and at times she'd felt as if she'd known him better before he'd knocked on her front door.

Livi frowned as she watched him pour enough syrup over his pancakes to make her teeth hurt.

"What?" Mitch grinned before offering her the bottle. "I left you some."

She blinked and shook her head. Brow still tight, she lifted a jar of fruit preserves before opening it and spreading a light layer over the golden crust of her pancake.

"I was married," she blurted out, the words surprising her as much as him.

Well, that took his attention off his pool of syrupy pancakes. She actually felt him come to attention from all the way across the small white table.

Setting his fork and knife on the sides of his plate, Mitch gave her his full attention.

She suddenly felt as if she'd stepped onto a stage in front of hundreds of people, all of whom were judging her body, her personality and even her morals.

Livi wanted to squirm. She'd rather her confession be

shrugged off with a good-natured smile, sort of like her preference for fruit over syrup had.

"How long were you married?"

"A couple of years." She made a show of cutting off a piece of pancake and eating it with exaggerated pleasure. He didn't take the hint. Just waited.

Livi grimaced and, with a regretful look at her breakfast, set her fork down. Preserves were best on hot pancakes. If she'd known they'd be delayed because of an uncomfortable conversation, she'd have stuck with syrup.

"My divorce was finalized in February, but we split over Christmas the previous year," she said. "It's old news, really."

"You must have been pretty young when you married."

"Twenty." She lifted her fork, but he was still giving her that intense peer-into-her-soul-and-scoop-out-secrets look. So she set the fork back down again and folded her hands in her lap. See, this would be a great time for her to be confident enough to tell him she didn't want to talk about it. She could say it was uncomfortable, tell him it wasn't a big deal and suggest he let it go.

So why didn't she? She'd wanted Mitch and she'd gone after him. She was a strong woman. A capable, intelligent, savvy person capable of standing up for what she wanted. Even if all she wanted was to avoid something.

Livi lifted her chin, deliberately picked up her fork again and cut a piece of pancake.

Then she sighed.

Maybe Mitch was right.

Maybe she really didn't have a lot of choice when it came to standing her ground. It certainly didn't feel as if she did.

"His name is Derrick. He's an athlete turned investment broker and he lives in New York now." What was she supposed to say? How did one describe an ex-husband to a new lover? This discussion had *socially awkward* written all over it.

"What happened?"

"Sometimes things just don't work out," she said with a shrug.

From Mitch's narrow-eyed look, that wasn't nearly enough information.

But nothing had a greater guarantee to send a man screaming into the night never to call again than a woman talking about infertility issues.

Admitting she'd been a gullible idiot who'd gotten fleeced didn't appeal a lot, either.

Then she thought of something safe to say and gave Mitch a big smile.

"He actually launched my career as a fitness expert."

"He inspired you to teach others to get in shape?"

"Well, no. I already had my degree and certifications and was working as a personal trainer when we met. He was a ball player, semipro, who'd come to me for training on the recommendation of some friends." Recommendation, dare—they were almost the same thing. "We'd only been married a few months when he was injured. He got the idea from his physical therapist, who'd just done a spot as an extra in a fitness video. One thing led to another. We formed Stripped Down Fitness and my new career was born."

Her words were upbeat and she knew her smile was perky and bright. It was her on-camera smile, after all.

But she felt as if Mitch's sharp eyes saw right through the cheer.

"The Fit To Be Naked videos? That seems like an odd thing for a man to encourage his wife to do."

Livi frowned. Was he judging her?

"And why is that?" she asked, stiffly.

Mitch obviously wasn't a highly trained special ops expert for nothing. He clued in immediately, his smile soothing as he reached across the table to take her hand.

Livi moved it out of reach.

"I'm not suggesting there's anything wrong with those videos, or with your involvement," he said carefully. "I simply don't know many men who would be comfortable with their wife being dubbed The Bump-and-Grind Queen."

"Would you?" Well, look at that. She *was* the type to stand her ground.

"I'm not married."

Her finger now tapping her plate, Livi silently tilted her head to the side and waited.

Mitch watched her with narrowed eyes before shrugging one shoulder.

"I'm not a jealous ass. I don't have a problem with others thinking the woman I'm with is sexy and desirable or knowing she's damned good at what she does," he said slowly, as if taking an extra moment to check each word for hidden explosives. "But isn't that the point? You're damned good at what you do. Didn't you have a strong reputation as a trainer before this series of videos? I suppose I'm simply surprised that your ex would choose to steer you in that particular direction."

That particular direction.

He obviously didn't mean training or producing videos. She was a little surprised he knew anything about her reputation pre–Fit To Be Naked, but at least he hadn't dug up the demise of that reputation. Her finger still tapping against the side of her plate, Livi debated explaining exactly how her once famous client list had been whittled down to a handful of strippers and a few housewives. But it was so difficult to know when the right time was to tell your current lover that your ex-husband had stolen from investors and left you holding the bag. That seemed like the kind of conversation that was better had over dinner. Not breakfast.

"Actually, it wasn't my ex who pulled together the Fit To Be Naked craze. All the credit for that goes to my current manager. Pole-dancing workouts were starting to take off and she saw a way to take the newest fitness craze to a higher level."

Tension tying knots in her stomach, Livi wanted to see what he'd say next. She wasn't ashamed of the direction her career had gone in. Had Billy Blanks been ashamed of combining kickboxing and fitness when he'd created Tae Bo? Was Beto Perez bumming over bringing Zumba to life? Of course not. Because they were effective, engaging workouts that provided more than just exercise. They offered inspiration. Maybe she was inspiring people to master a hip thrust instead of an uppercut, but the results were the same. They were captivated enough to stick with the program and see results.

"I'd say you must have jumped quite a few levels to get where you are now. It takes some major connections to make an impression on the US Navy," he told her with a laugh.

The knots in her stomach loosened a little.

"Maybe. Or maybe I just have a well-connected manager." Or well-connected aunt. Or—Livi remembered the conspiratorial look between Roz and her mom—probably a combination of the two.

"That'd be the manager you called 'pushy'?" he asked with a smile. Since he finally picked up his fork again and started eating, Livi managed to smile back.

"That'd be her. She's pretty amazing. Intimidating." Especially if you were her daughter. "I don't think there's anything she's set her sights on that she hasn't managed to pull off."

"Maybe I should thank her for the idea for the SEAL workout, then," he teased. Then his expression turned serious, watchful. "It sounds as if she's done some great things for your career. Do you prefer her direction to the one your ex had you on?"

Prefer? Livi frowned. Nobody had ever asked her that. Pauline had taken her higher. But Derrick had taken responsibility for launching her. She wondered where she factored into their calculations.

Since saying that would sound whiny, she just shrugged.

"You're doing a different workout than the one you showed me, though, aren't you?" she asked instead, figuring changing the subject completely was much better than tiptoeing around what wouldn't be said.

Mitch's frown made her wonder if she'd have been better off tiptoeing.

"Why would you say I'm doing a different workout than the one I gave you?"

"I was just making conversation." Brows tight, Livi shrugged. "I didn't mean to suggest anything."

And she really hadn't meant to irritate him. Especially since her pancakes were now cold and his chest looked so hot. She'd been starting to have a few ideas for a breakfast substitute. Maybe her shyness wasn't a drawback, Livi mulled with a sigh. Maybe it was a warning that she'd be better off keeping her mouth shut most of the time.

He barely shifted, just setting his elbows on either side of his all-but-licked-clean plate. His expression was mild, his eyes calm. But her stomach clenched tightly, because Livi felt as if he'd pulled on battle gear.

"I didn't think you were making a negative suggestion," he said, his smile friendly. How did he do that? She knew he was upset, or at the very least, disturbed. Yet he managed to look upbeat and calm. It was freaky.

"I'm just curious why you'd think I'm not following the workout."

"I wasn't implying that you're not working out," she said

quickly, waving her hand in the air. "You're in great shape. It's obvious that you work out regularly."

Neither her words nor her big, cheesy smile had any effect on him. The pleasant smile stayed, the calm interest in his eyes didn't flicker. And he still had that intense, I-know-thousands-of-ways-of-making-you-talk vibe going on.

Livi shoved her hand through her sleep-tousled hair and tried to figure out at which exact point this morning had taken a sharp turn toward hell.

But she couldn't think with Mitch staring at her like that.

"Your muscles are structured differently," she said, the words rushing out to bounce between them. "The workout you outlined, the one you talked about—it's well-balanced and hits all the muscle groups hard. But a part of the series focuses more deeply on the lats than on the biceps."

Mitch shook his head. He'd lost the laser look and now just seemed confused.

"If you'd been doing that particular workout, your lats, your upper back, would be tighter. Don't get me wrong," she said quickly, her eyes huge as she waved one hand to shoo aside any offense he might take. "You're in incredible condition. But if you'd been working your upper back that intensively, you wouldn't be so stiff, since the muscles wouldn't have mended completely."

"You're saying I'm too stiff?"

Livi peered at him, trying to decide if that was a double entendre.

"Not *too* stiff. Simply healed," she said carefully. "That program you showed me included a lot of emphasis on weighted pull-ups, often using another man's bodyweight. That sort of giant-set routine would mean you were consistently pushing your lat muscles past the point of fatigue and giving them very little time to heal. Or harden. Yours are solid, but I noticed last night that your thigh muscles are tense."

"Did you?" he murmured, his wicked grin offering its own double entendre.

Livi's lips twitched, but she didn't smile. Instead, she leaned forward, her hands fisted in her lap. She wasn't sure why, but it was suddenly vital he understood that she knew what she was doing. That he respected that her career was about more than teaching sexy women how to fold a dollar bill with their butt cheeks.

"I'm guessing you've shifted your workout program to be something that puts a lot of stress on your glutes and hamstrings. Probably intervals that focus on climbing and running on the beach, if I had to guess."

His smile spread, slow and pleased. Mitch pushed away from the table, this time not giving her a chance to move her hand before he grabbed it. He pulled her to her feet and right into his arms.

"Damn, you're good. I've worked with some top fitness pros in my day, but you could kick all their asses," he told her, right before he lifted her into his arms and took her mouth.

He'd just swept her off her feet. Literally. Livi melted at the romance of it, even as her pride sang a little at his words. His tongue swept over hers then, and everything—romance, pride, worry—all faded into a hazy glow of passion.

How THE HELL had she made it seem so easy?

Mitch glared at the pot of funky-looking milk, tilting it this way then that and watching the top layer ripple like thin plastic.

That couldn't be good.

He glanced at the waiting mug, its chocolate shavings already heaped in and ready, then at the milk scum, and debated. Maybe it wouldn't be that bad. He wouldn't give it to Livi, of course, but he could try it himself, just to see. He might have even come up with a new delicacy.

Chocolate milk-scum surprise.

He dipped his finger in the still scalding hot liquid then and gingerly tasted it.

The surprise would be keeping it down, he decided with a grimace before dumping it in the sink and starting over. Clean pot, fresh milk… What else?

He tried to remember what Livi had done when she'd made it, but the details were hazed by all the lusty memories. Or more likely, because he'd been more focused on what she'd said—or hadn't said—about the holidays than he had in learning the nuances of not ruining milk.

He was pretty sure she'd had a spoon, though.

Mitch grabbed one, this time putting the heat on medium-low instead of high. Stirring the cold milk—maybe that helped keep it from getting gross as it heated—he thought back to Livi's description of her holiday.

She'd said her ex had left the previous Christmas, but she'd spent the one before in Vail. Had he been with her? Livi wasn't the brag-about-one-man-while-with-another type, but he'd still come away with the impression that she'd been alone.

Who the hell left their wife alone on Christmas?

Sure, it happened a lot in the military, but only when a guy was on assignment. A guy would have to be a major douche to leave his pretty young wife hanging alone on the ski slopes for the holidays.

Then again, he'd ended their marriage the next year at the holidays, so maybe he was closer to a captain douche than a major.

Grinning a little at his lame joke, Mitch watched the milk start to form tiny bubbles around the edges of the pot.

He had no problem hating the guy on principle, but he

had a feeling that once he started digging, he'd find plenty of other reasons to hate him just fine.

Starting with putting that look of doubt in Livi's eyes.

Not the shyness. Mitch recognized that for what it was now. Even though they'd spent the last week inside her apartment, mostly naked, just the two of them delighting in the pleasures of each other's bodies...

Mitch frowned. What had he been thinking about again?

Oh, yeah.

Livi was shy.

He knew her tells now. She put on a bright smile, a little too bright, when she was nervous. She had amazing control of her body language—he didn't know if that was because of her vocation or her time in front of the camera—so she'd look perfectly relaxed and at ease. But her fingers always gave her away. Flexing and moving if she thought they were hidden, clenched tight if she couldn't tuck them away.

Those videos—hell, the eight-month cross-country tour she'd done to promote the videos—those must have been hell for her. She'd brushed it off when he'd said as much, calling it a learning experience that had had more benefits than shortcomings.

She'd said it was her new manager who'd put her front and center in those videos. Call it a hunch, but Mitch was pretty sure her ex had had some role in that, too.

That she was better off without him went without saying.

Still, Mitch wouldn't mind if she had a few things to say. There were details he'd like to know. Things he was curious about.

He'd watched a lot of marriages fall apart, had always figured it was as much an occupational hazard as, well, being shot at. Yeah, it was a risk, but the results could be mitigated with a little forethought.

A solid marriage? It could be done.

He'd seen it done.

And if it could be done in the military, it could damned well be done by a civilian with a classy wife like Livi.

Not that he was thinking crazy thoughts like marriage. Not in the he-was-ready-to-do-it sense. More like… curious musings about how it worked. Nothing wrong with curiosity.

Mitch tested the milk with his finger again and pulled a satisfied face. Not bad this time.

He poured it over the chocolate shavings then stirred, careful not to slop it over the edges of Livi's pretty purple mugs. He wondered if she realized her entire apartment was decorated in ocean hues. Calm, soothing ocean hues. He wouldn't mind adding a little of her other moods, sharp cobalt and the edgy white of the storm-swept seas. Would Livi go for that? He had a gorgeous glass dish he'd picked up in Corfu years ago because it had reminded him of lightning on the water. Maybe he'd send it to her for Christmas.

Mitch grabbed a can from the refrigerator and gave it a good shake, then popped the lid and added a hefty spray of white foam to the top of one of the mugs. Figuring he'd keep her company, he added it to the second one, too.

He grabbed a couple of the candy canes he'd picked up in his store run. He looked at the whipped-cream-heaped mugs, then at the cellophane-wrapped candy, and weighed his options. Going with the easiest route, he simply crushed them in his fist, poured the peppermint dust into his other palm and threw away the wrapper.

No wonder his mom had gone the "toss a cup of water in the microwave then stir in brown powder" route.

Some things were worth the extra work.

He tried his hand at fancy, sprinkling the crushed candy cane over the whipped cream in a heart shape. He tilted his head to the side and frowned. It looked like Texas. He sprinkled a little more to fill it in and called that one his.

And went a little slower doing the next one.

Some people were worth the extra effort.

"Are you having fun?"

Mitch didn't start. His pulse barely changed. But damn, she'd surprised him.

He glanced over his shoulder, a warm smile spreading at the sight of Livi. Her hair was a sleep-rumpled curtain of gold, falling over her robe like the sun against the ocean. The silk fabric skimmed, cupped and accented, reminding him of the perfection beneath.

"I made you a treat," he said, lifting both mugs and turning to offer her one.

"I thought I smelled chocolate," she said with a sleepy laugh as she took hers. Her eyes went soft and her mouth rounded in a soft O before she pressed trembling lips together and gave him a tremulous look.

Mitch cringed. She had that look women got before they burst into tears and claimed they were happy. He didn't care what they called them—tears were tears and they sucked.

"You're so sweet," she said after a moment. Thankfully she said it in a tone with plenty of happy but no tears in evidence.

"You haven't tasted it yet," he warned. Then, because that's the kind of guy he was, he took the first sip to make sure it wasn't dangerous to her palate. Hot, sweet and just a little crunchy. Maybe he should have stirred the chocolate longer? Still, it wasn't bad.

"It's wonderful," Livi told him, running her tongue over her upper lip to catch all the whipped cream. "You're wonderful."

"No arguing with that," Mitch decided, gesturing to the living room. Once they were settled on the couch, Livi's long legs crossed over his lap, he took another drink and initiated maneuvers. Let Operation Information commence. "I'm not sure this is what you meant by peppermint in your chocolate, though."

"It's fabulous." Her eyes locked on his. Livi speared her tongue through the white cream and candy bits and curled it into her mouth. Damn, she had a good tongue. Getting hot and hard, especially with her feet rubbing against his thighs and climbing higher by the second, Mitch accepted the challenge. She had a way of fogging his brain, but he wanted information. This was a good time to test whether he could work through the fog.

"I know it's not topped with that home-whipped cream you talked about, but is it at least close to what you remembered?" he prompted. All he needed was the opening. As soon as she gave it to him, he'd be able to find out everything he wanted.

Livi didn't give him the opening. She didn't even respond. Her face a study of conflicts—surprise, delight, worry and frustration—she deprived his lap of her feet, set her mug on the table and got up to cross the room.

"When did you get this?" she asked quietly, her back to him.

Mitch didn't have to see around her to know what she was looking at. He'd set the little potted pine on her dining table before he'd started the hot chocolate.

"When I got the canned whipped cream and candy canes." Mitch got to his feet, but didn't cross the room.

Unlike her tongue trick telling him how she'd felt about those, he couldn't read how she felt about the tree. He'd thought she'd love it. He'd actually been anticipating a little wild thank-you sex.

He heard her take a deep breath and decided to kiss that anticipation goodbye.

Then she turned to face him.

Mitch had faced a lot of things in his life, and he always faced them head-on. He specialized in danger, reveled in finding ways to overcome odds. He was the best for a reason... He was trained to be.

In that moment, for the first time in his life, Mitch knew what it was like to want to turn tail and run.

"Thank you." She stepped forward, arms coming up as if to launch herself at him.

"Uh." He held up one hand out to stop her. "You don't come near me if you're doing that. You wanna have sex, I'm your man. You want to fight and argue, I'll step right up. You need to get advice, to talk, to have someone killed, I can arrange that. But you cannot and will not cry on me."

"But you are so sweet," she said, adding a few extra syllables to the last word because she was trying to catch her breath.

The couch pressed against the back of his calves, reminding him that jumping over it and running would be truly pathetic.

"Livi, can you imagine having to get on stage in front of a few thousand people and give a speech? Totally unprepared, out of the blue, on a subject you don't know?"

Her tears stopped, but her breath didn't even out. If anything, it got shakier. Eyes wide in horror and her skin going chalky against the tear tracks, she shuddered.

"That's how I feel seeing you cry," he said quietly.

"Ah." She glanced at the tree again and stared at the floor for a few moments before meeting his eyes. When she did, hers were clear, her smile was calm and, other than the faint sheen of damp on her cheeks, her demeanor was completely tear-free. "Sorry. I've never had anyone get me a tree before, so it took me by surprise."

And there it was.

His opening.

Relaxing, ready to move on with the mission, Mitch settled back on the couch. Then he saw the bottom part of her robe fluttering, her fingers clenching and unclenching the fabric behind her back.

She was doing the same thing she did with her shyness.

Suppressing it, hiding it. Probably suffering for it.

"C'mere," Mitch said with a sigh, getting to his feet again. When she shook her head, he simply crooked his finger.

Livi pressed her lips together, glanced over her shoulder at the tree and flew into his arms with a sob. Mitch's gut clenched, but he ignored it as he ran soothing hands over her back.

She cried silently. Hot, wet tears soaked his shoulder. Other than her breath, and the fingers clutching, unclutching, then clutching his back again, she barely moved.

But he felt as if she were falling apart.

Over the tiny Christmas tree? Or something else?

Whatever it was, she only cried for a minute or two, thank God. Then she pulled it all back in with a deep breath.

"I thought tears freaked you out," she said, giving him a questioning look through damp eyes.

Mitch pressed her face back to his chest. It wasn't as bad if he didn't have to see the tears. At least, that's what he was going to tell himself.

"That's no reason for you to hide your reaction. You've got a right to feel whatever you feel. Why should you pretend otherwise? I'm a big boy, I'll deal."

This time when Livi looked at him, it was to give him a frown.

"But now I know it bothers you, I just won't cry over things."

"You mean you'll put my comfort over your own feelings? That'd make me a total ass with major control issues," Mitch said with a dismissive laugh. "Babe, you embrace whatever you're feeling. Good or bad, it should be up to you to feel it and decide if you want to go with it or not. That's nobody else's call."

Mitch was ready to give himself a nice pat on the back

for that little pep talk in spite of his tear phobia. Then he caught the look in her eyes.

A baffled sort of pain, as if she didn't understand his words. Or, he realized with a sigh, couldn't quite let herself believe them.

Looked like he didn't need to hate her ex on principle alone. He had a thousand reasons, all of them right there in her pained expression.

Well.

Mitch let emotions slide through him, not bothering to name or try to analyze them right now. He'd do that later.

Operation Information had taken a major turn. The kind of turn that would force him to ask himself some questions. Again, later.

Right now, he had one simple choice.

He knew Livi would appease his curiosity. But while that'd make him feel good, he knew it wouldn't do the same for her.

Mitch rubbed his knuckles over Livi's cheek, marveling in her sweet face. He had to leave at dawn to catch a flight home for Christmas. He could leave his questions unanswered until he saw her again. But he wouldn't leave without giving her something to smile about.

"You know," he said slowly, shifting his body just a little to bring his in more perfect alignment. "I actually do like hearing you cry sometimes."

"You what?" She frowned, the hurt taking a backseat to the irritation.

"It's a special kind of cry," Mitch told her, brushing his lips over hers at the same time his knuckles skimmed down the front of her robe, brushing her nipples. "A pleasured cry."

"Is that so?" Her eyes darkened again, this time with amused pleasure.

"It is. And I think you owe me a cry or two." He used

his palm this time to cup her breast, delighting in the instant puckering of her nipple beneath his hand.

"I owe you?" She shifted her hips, rubbing erotically against the already erect length of his dick.

"I made you hot chocolate," he reminded her.

"Mmm, you did." Livi's smile was wicked and sweet at the same time. "I wonder if there's any whipped cream left."

"I got two cans," Mitch said as he swept her into his arms.

_10_

THREE HOURS AND two rocking orgasms later, Mitch was pretty sure he'd rode the whipped-cream-induced sugar high for all it was worth. All he wanted to do was fall into a gratified crash and sleep it off. But he couldn't.

Sometimes a man just had to do what a man had to do.

And Mitch had to get up.

Not his dick—that had been up and down so many times this week it might as well have had its own elevator.

His body.

Up, out of bed.

Up, out of Livi's apartment.

Up, out of the state of California, even.

But… He didn't want to move.

Mitch couldn't remember ever feeling as good as he did now.

Not physically, though his body was so drugged with pleasure he could barely move.

Not mentally, though his mind filled with facts, impressions and even more questions about Livi. He'd talked with her more in the last three days than he figured he'd talked to any woman in his life, outside of relatives.

Not emotionally.

Putting the brakes on that train of thought, Mitch frowned at the ceiling. Livi's holiday lights slowly faded from blue to purple to pink, the colors' glow dimming as the room grew lighter.

Maybe they hadn't known each other long. It'd only been a handful of phone calls, then three days of talking and making love. Of cooking meals together and making love. Laughing and sharing, joking and sleeping together—between making love.

But what did time matter? She'd touched him like nobody else in his life ever had.

Was that love?

Mitch's eyes flew open, the foggy dregs of sleep shattering. His stomach clenched. He was fascinated by her, but that didn't mean it was some heavy emotional thing.

He couldn't imagine not seeing her again, and was already missing the feel of her in his arms even though she hadn't left them. She was a gorgeous, sexy woman. That was to be expected.

And sure, he'd opened up with her more than he ever had with a woman. But that was because she was so easy to talk to, so curious and supportive and sweet.

See. There was no reason to start thinking crazily.

His attraction to spending more time—a lot more time—with Livi was all very justified. Almost tidily so. He knew that anything that tidily organized on the surface was either a facade, or camouflage for a hot mess of some kind.

Which brought him full circle, right back to that wild emotional thinking. If he wasn't careful, he was going to be in deep trouble.

"I have to go," he said aloud. *Nice.* He grimaced at the ceiling. *Great way to break the news.*

"I might be able to move in a few decades," Livi mumbled into the mattress where she lay, facedown. The emerald-green satin sheet pooled over her thighs just below the sweet curve of her butt.

Unable to resist, Mitch rolled onto his side to enjoy the view. Her skin melted from creamy white to pale gold just there at the small of her back, a subtle tan line so smooth he wondered if she went nude part of the time.

His body hardened—again—at the image of Livi on a beach, her bare body running across the surf.

"I can come back on the twenty-sixth," he said, not caring that his family would pitch a fit. They'd get over it. "We can spend New Year's Eve together."

He liked the idea of ringing in a new year with her. The possibilities stretched way beyond just champagne, midnight kisses and Livi's sweet body wrapped in a sexy little dress.

Although there was a lot to be said for sexy little dresses. Reaching over, Mitch slid the palm of his hand up her spine and back down again. Her silky skin was warm, the muscles beneath lax. Damn, she had the most perfect body.

"Actually I leave right after Christmas," she said into the pillow, disappointment coloring her words. "I'm booked on a cruise or four."

Mitch blinked.

"Or four?"

Livi slowly shifted her head to the side, peeking at him from under a swath of hair.

"I'm booked for a month, but I think it's actually four different trips. You know, out of Florida around the Caribbean, then back to Florida to exchange passengers before doing it all over again."

"You're working on the cruise ship," he said, realization dawning on him. He reached over to slide his finger along her bicep, scooping up her silken hair to tuck it to the side so he could see her face. "So it's business, not pleasure?"

"Both, maybe," she said, her words slurred with exhaustion. As the cause of her lack of sleep, Mitch knew he should feel bad. But it'd felt too damned good. "A lot of my regulars will be there, a few strippers, JoyBoy the Drag Queen and the church girls."

JoyBoy the Drag Queen? And the church girls? What in the hell did she do with her regulars? Mitch angled himself onto his elbow to get a closer look at her face to see if she was kidding.

Nope.

Not kidding.

Not even awake.

Deciding to ask her later, he glanced at the sun and guessed that it was around six in the morning. He really did have to go, but it was so hard to tear himself away. He did a quick calculation, figuring how long it'd take to get to the airport from here if he skipped stopping by base to get his things.

Long enough for another hug, he thought. Carefully wrapping his arms around her, he pulled Livi tight against him. She murmured something, more a purr than actual words, and snuggled closer.

Damn, he was going to miss her.

Never before had he questioned leaving a place, a person.

Never once had he wished to be anywhere except where he was, whether that meant sweating in the deserts of Iraq, freezing in the waters of the Arctic, or once—as much as he'd have liked to forget—carrying a recovered SEAL's body through mortar fire to bring him to his final resting place in Arlington.

Mitch didn't believe in regrets and didn't bother second-guessing. He always lived in the moment, because that's what he had.

He pressed a kiss against the top of Livi's head. Breathing deeply, he drew in her scent, letting it fill him with the sweet delight that was Livi.

He was forced to admit with a sinking feeling that those peacefully conflict-free days might be numbered.

"C'mon, Liv. Let's hit the clubs. They have a good one called the Captain's Deck. The Lido Club is retro and fun to look at, but the music bites. There's a fogey club, you know, the kind with ballroom dancing and dapper old guys. We could hit them all if you want, or go straight for the Captain's Deck and see the hottest guys."

As Tessa went on and on about the hot guys, Livi wondered if she should have stayed in the shower a little longer. She coated her skin with lotion before sliding into her robe, the movements difficult in the tiny bathroom. Being one of the starring attractions of an All New You cruise that featured fitness, motivation and healthy lifestyle programs earned you a balcony stateroom, but not a luxury bathroom.

Was it like this on the ships Mitch served on? Not specifically—she was sure the Navy sleeping quarters weren't wallpapered with bright purple and orange flowers. But the sense of being in a cocoon, all compact and closed in and secure.

She'd have to ask him. Anticipation curled like smoke low in her belly, ready to ignite into flame as soon as she heard his voice. So far they'd only been texting since Christmas, but he'd asked if she'd be available to do a video chat tonight. And oh, boy, would she.

"C'mon, Liv," Tessa shouted from the other room. "Let's check out the ship's party life."

"How do you know all of these things?" Livi asked her, coming out of the bathroom in her robe, rubbing a towel over her just washed hair. "You've been in here sick ever since we boarded the ship. You're only getting through the workout sessions by doping with antihistamines—then you come back here and snore."

"I do not snore," Tessa objected. Then she gave Livi a horrified look. "Do I? I've never taken pills for seasickness before. Who knows what they're doing to me. Do I drool, too? Please, tell me I don't drool."

Snickering at her friend's frantic tone, Livi sank onto her own bed, the twin of Tessa's, and combed her fingers through her wet tangles. She was tempted to tease, but she knew how rough the last five days had been on her friend. Knowing Tessa's vanity, if she thought she was anything less than sexy and sophisticated under the influence of the pills, she'd quit taking them. It was only after Livi had poined out that puking wasn't sexy either that she'd tried them in the first place.

"You don't drool," Livi assured her. Seeing the concern on Tessa's face—which was a smidge less green now—she lifted her hand in promise. "No snoring, either."

Looking oddly young with her face bare and her hair pulled back with a headband, Tessa gave a relieved sigh. Then with a hint of her usual verve, she shifted onto her knees on the vivid pink coverlet and spread her hands.

"Well, then? Wanna party tonight? We can start with the guys in the fogey club—those old ones love to buy pretty girls drinks. We'll work our way up to the Captain's Deck and let this guy show us his dance moves. His name is Miguel and he's got the sweetest butt on the entire ship."

Even if Livi didn't have plans to sneak off to some private corner of the ship with her cell phone and talk dirty with Mitch, none of that would have appealed to her.

"So you scoped all of that out between the end of our three o'clock Pole Power workout and my getting out of the shower?"

"I have my ways," Tessa declared grandly. At Livi's mischievous look, she grinned and admitted, "JoyBoy. He's hit all the clubs at least twice and made a list of the hottest single guys on the ship. He said we could have the straight ones."

"Because he's taking all the rest?" Livi laughed in delight. If anyone could handle it, the six-foot-four beanpole of a redhead could.

"That was sweet of him, but you can have my share," she told Tessa.

"I don't want your share. I don't even want my share."

Tessa scowled, flopping backward onto the bed. Her *Just Do Me* tee rode up, baring her belly above simple black yoga pants. "We can dress up. I'll watch you eat in a fancy restaurant and we'll go dance with each other and ring in the New Year. I just want to get out of this room."

Livi hadn't told Tessa about her and Mitch.

At first it'd just been phone calls, and she hadn't wanted to hear the lectures on how lousy military guys were or how no guy was worth the drama Pauline would create when she found out. Then, after things really heated up, Livi figured things between her and Mitch wouldn't last long, so why tell anyone? This way it was just hers. Hers and Mitch's.

Besides, Tessa knew her too well. If Livi told her about the relationship, Tessa would start asking questions. She'd talk about emotions and repercussions and all that crazy stuff. For a self-proclaimed sex kitten, Tessa was pretty uptight about some things.

All of which meant that Livi's plans for the evening wouldn't get her out of the party invite. So she started to offer an excuse instead.

That she was tired, which wasn't really true.

Or that she hadn't packed any party dresses. Which was.

Oh, her mother had told her to, saying there was plenty of networking to be done. Since Pauline had an unexpected deal come up, she'd insisted her daughter glad-hand and socialize in her place. The idea of having to play nicey-nice with a bunch of strangers over and over again had put Livi into a cold sweat even as she'd pulled evening wear out to pack.

Then she'd remembered what Mitch had said about embracing her feelings and deciding how she wanted to handle them. Since the idea of doing cocktail-party promotions made her feel nauseous, she'd put every single dress right back in the closet.

She'd felt good about it at the time. Strong and empowered. Now, though…

"Do you think I'm doing a lousy job representing Stripped Down Fitness?" she asked Tessa. "That hanging out here with you or chilling with a few people by the pool is a waste of this opportunity?"

"What?" It only took a moment for the baffled confusion to clear from Tessa's face. "Oh, screw that. You're teaching five sessions every day, you stay after each one and visit until the last person leaves, and you're on deck the rest of the time being friendly. How's that slacking off?"

"Pauline is worried," Livi admitted with a shrug. "The Fit To Be Naked sales have plateaued, so she's sure they'll plummet soon."

"Right little ray of sunshine, your mom."

"Isn't she just?"

"Are things really that bad? I thought that's why you— we—did that tour earlier this year. To push video and franchise sales and hit that plateau. Did something change?"

"You mean did another creditor or bilked investor pop up?" Livi shook her head. "No. I'm solvent and sound. I mean, the company will still be paying back the loans for another couple of years, but we should be fine. I was just feeling guilty about skipping the parties."

"Are you sure?" Tessa asked, her expression just as suspicious as her tone. "Do you need me to stay on? Like I told Pauline, my schedule is flexible. I can make myself available after the cruise."

"No." Livi dropped onto the bed next to Tessa to give her a quick hug.

"You've done so much this last year. I couldn't have gotten through that tour or those video shoots without you. I totally appreciate your help. But Stripped Down Fitness is really okay." When that didn't ease the concern on Tessa's face, Livi added, "I'm putting together a new program based on the Navy SEAL workout. I've got plenty of one-on-one clients and if things get tight, I can pick up a few group sessions here or there. I'm finally where I want to be," Livi assured her. "Don't worry about Pauline. You know how she is. Every cloud has another cloud behind it."

She frowned, playing back Tessa's words.

"When did Pauline check your availability?" she asked. Granted, Tessa was her go-to workout partner and had starred in all of the Stripped Down Fitness videos—Livi was sure she was one of the main reasons for their huge success. But other than promotional events like the tour or this cruise, she wasn't a trainer. As Tessa liked to put it, she was all about the window dressing.

"When she called two weeks ago to confirm the cruise details she asked about my availability into February." Tessa grimaced. "I knew you were hoping to ease off the big promotions so I kept it vague."

Livi's stomach clenched, dread tiptoeing with sneaky fingers down her spine. Pauline was up to something. She'd been extra friendly when Livi joined her for Christmas dinner, she'd blown off this cruise for a meeting, and now she was tapping Tessa's team for availability?

Not live television, Livi prayed. She'd hoped the idea of this new workout direction had been enough to derail Pauline from that particular train of thought. She'd been so hopeful, she'd never actually told her mother that she hated the idea and didn't want to do it.

Needing to move, to shake off the conflicting feelings in her belly, Livi got up and paced. The stateroom was so small, though, that she could only take four steps either way.

Tessa watched the glinting ocean through their balcony door for a moment before asking, "What do you think she's up to?"

Livi frowned, not sure.

"We'll be making a video of the SEAL workout, but so far I've only outlined my program ideas." And made copious notes of how incredibly beneficial the real SEAL program was—both for the men using it and for the women delighting in the results. Mitch's body was a work of art and the things he did with it... Oh, my.

She didn't think she wanted those in a video, though.

At least, not one available to the public.

"I have to finish adapting their workout to be doable by civilians. Then I'll test it myself for a month or so to adjust and record the results," she murmured, thinking through the process aloud as she paced. "I need to create modifications, pull together a control group to test the workout with and adjust again. At that point, we should be ready to film."

There was more to it, of course. Things like set design, costuming and film crew. But Pauline handled all of that.

"I wonder if anyone knows how much work you put into these workouts," Tessa mused. "Even the ones you don't film take you months to develop and fine-tune before you teach them."

"If someone is paying for my expertise, they deserve the best I can give them." Livi shrugged, wishing her best was enough. She'd love to give up the parts that she sucked at.

She thought about Tessa's question on the state of Stripped Down Fitness. Another three years and those loans would be paid. Livi wouldn't—couldn't—say it aloud. It'd be totally unappreciative and ungrateful. But in her secret heart of hearts, she dreamed that someday after she'd paid off the company's debt, she could just let it go. No more videos, no more tours, no more big crowds.

She wouldn't, of course. Too many people, including Tessa, had invested too much in her success.

"Whatever she's up to, it can't be that bad," Tessa said encouragingly as she got to her feet. "You gave your mom very specific limits on what you would do this year and as much as she likes to act otherwise, it is your company."

But that assurance did little to settle the worry in Livi's stomach.

CHOCOLATE OR ROSES?

Mitch couldn't decide.

Both were pretty traditional Valentine's Day gifts. Was traditional lame? Nah. But unimaginative, maybe.

Should he go a different route? Or just find some way to give traditional a little more appeal? Did she like roses? He'd have to find out. He still had time. He'd get her favorite flowers and ask Romeo where to get the best chocolate. Something decadent and fancy.

Something that would taste amazing when he licked it off Livi's silken body. He imagined her lying on her bed surrounded by rose petals, the moonlight glinting off her bare skin. He'd drizzle it over the fullness of her breasts, watching as it slid down her body. And then he'd follow the path with his tongue.

Or better yet, he'd fill her tub with chocolate syrup.

Mitch grinned. Now *that* was imaginative.

"Donovan!"

Damn.

Mitch blinked to clear the fantasy from his brain and saw the small desert village, smoke billowing as flames poured out the windows across from him.

Growling low in his throat, he dropped his head, his helmet making a dull thud against the adobe wall.

"You wanna haul out the dead bodies now? Or wait until you're finished with your little daydream?" Captain Mahoney's voice buzzed with irritation through Mitch's headset.

The CSAR trainer was a hard-ass who hated slackers, and Mitch knew he'd be paying for his inattention. As he should. Combat Search and Rescue was serious and deserved 110 percent of his focus. Mitch and his team were here to train, but also to look at integrating new elements into their own expanded training program.

A program that required focus, damn it.

"You back with us, Donovan?"

"Yes, sir," he responded tightly.

"Initiate rescue."

"Initiating," he muttered through clenched teeth.

Mitch allowed himself one last vicious curse before putting it aside. Shutting out all outside thoughts, closing down any random emotions, he spent the next ten minutes doing what he was here to do. Find his men.

The last one was deep inside a flaming hovel of a building. Mitch needed to crawl on his belly and blow up a wall to rescue him.

Mitch crouched in the tiny cellar, giving the lounging man a long look.

"You dead?"

"Nah. I'm invincible," Romeo said with a grin. But the timer on his helmet showed that invincible wouldn't have held out against Mitch's distraction.

Mitch didn't say a word. Just hefted his failure onto his shoulders along with Romeo's body and headed out of the smoke-filled room.

Twenty minutes later, rescue effected, orders issued, his team changed gear for the next round and Mitch glanced at Romeo.

"Better it happen in training," his friend said quietly.

Mitch's jaw worked. Romeo was trying to cut him a break.

"Better it didn't happen at all."

"We train, we practice, we hone and we perfect. We're the best of the best and we dedicate ourselves to that." Gabriel looked out over the Nevada desert, his eyes unfathomable. "But in the end, we're all at the mercy of one simple reality."

"Is this where you tell me the reality is that we're all human? To accept that we can't be perfect or that everyone makes a mistake?" Ripping his helmet off, Mitch swiped a hand over his head and gave his friend a hard look.

"What? No way." Looking insulted, Romeo shook his head. "I'm going into battle with you. I expect you to be inhumanly perfect with no freaking mistakes. That's my ass on the line next to you, bro."

His jaw tight, Mitch took the well-deserved smackdown. He didn't offer an excuse. He didn't apologize or promise to do better.

"So what's the reality?" he finally asked.

"The reality is that we're men. And even the best of the best men have dicks. We're led by them." With that piece of profound wisdom, and a slap on the back, Romeo grabbed his gear.

Dumbfounded, it took Mitch a few moments to do the same.

As they made their way through the naval air base to the next round of maneuvers, Mitch muttered, "I'm not being led by my dick."

"Sure, you are," Romeo shot back cheerfully. Then, just before they reached the others, he stopped and gave Mitch an intense look. "Just be careful, Irish. You're standing on a cliff right now. You've got good balance, but if you fall, you lose."

"Lose what?"

"That's the problem. You never know till you hit the ground."

MITCH WAS STILL considering Romeo's words two days later when he joined his grandfather for lunch. Distinguished in his dark blue suit, Admiral Walter Donovan fit right in with the upscale country-club-style restaurant. The visit had been a surprise—straight off the training field, Mitch's fatigues didn't blend nearly as well.

That his grandfather was in civilian clothes meant this was a personal visit. That he'd flown in to a remote air base to have it said he felt it was a priority.

The tension tightening the back of Mitch's neck warned him to proceed with caution.

"I'm surprised to see you on the west coast again so soon," Mitch said after they'd placed their orders.

"Some things are best discussed in person."

Ah. Good. Mitch leaned back in his chair, glad they'd be getting right to the point. He hated when these things took until dessert.

"Such as?"

"As you know, no man is alone in the military. Our strengths come from careful planning, considered choices and, yes, the occasional sacrifice." His avuncular smile indicating this was a good ol' grandfather-to-grandson chat, the Admiral shrugged. "It's come to my attention there might be some factors that need to be addressed going forward. Mistakes that need to be rectified, if you will."

For the most part, Mitch had led an exemplary career. His record was spotless, his reputation the same. That someone had seen fit to tattle to his grandfather that he'd lost focus on a training mission was pathetic enough. But that it had mandated an in-person discussion was ridiculous.

"You're a valuable asset to your country, and as such, you can't make the same choices other men do. Not if you're going to reach your full potential," the Admiral continued to pontificate. "Now, as a man, I understand, but as your grandfather, as your mentor, I do think it'd be in your best interest to remove yourself from certain temptations."

What the hell?

"Wait." Mitch held up his hand. "You're talking about my relationship with Olivia Kane?"

"I prefer to call it an association."

"Call it what you want. It's a relationship." His eyes locked on the older man's, Mitch leaned forward. "A serious relationship."

"So my resources indicate."

"Resources?" Mitch scowled. "My mother has squids spying on me?"

"Your mother is concerned—rightfully so—that you might make an ill-advised choice that will not only impact your happiness but your career."

"This is the same mother whose been trying to marry me off since I turned legal age?"

And then it hit him.

"The ill-advised choice being associating with the wrong person," he stated. "She doesn't approve of Livi."

"She has legitimate concerns." Seeing the stubborn jut of Mitch's chin, his grandfather tilted his head. "The woman in question is divorced. Her name is linked with strippers. And she makes her living in the entertainment industry. While there were no charges filed, her company was involved in shady practices with investors a few years back. Those, young man, are facts worth being concerned over."

How dare he judge Livi? Fury surged in Mitch. He held his clenched fists beneath the table, trying to keep all of his anger in check.

"Facts, sir?" Mitch carefully smoothed his thoughts, knowing that emotional reactions were often a fatal luxury in battle. "From my perspective, your interpretation of the information at hand is somewhat biased."

"Is that what you think?" With just a shift of his shoulders, the Admiral traded avuncular grandfather for superior officer. For the first time he could recall, Mitch resented it. If advice didn't work, orders would? That was fine when it came to his career. But this was his personal life. "You're about to join the most prestigious and powerful Special

Missions Unit in the world. This isn't the time to be distracted by a woman, especially one who brings so little to your career."

Anger, irritation, outrage—none of which he'd ever felt toward his grandfather before—now pounded through his system. But he refused to discuss Livi or his private life in this context. If the Admiral wanted to have an official conversation, that's what they'd have.

"I made it to the selection phase for DEVGRU. That doesn't mean I've been invited to attend operations training," Mitch corrected meticulously. "Nor does it mean that if invited, I'll choose to go."

"Because of this woman."

"Because I'm not sure it's where I'd do the most good." And yeah, although Mitch would take a bullet to the gut before he'd admit it to his grandfather, because of Livi. "The program we're developing in covert operations is one I'm passionate about, one I have a lot to contribute to and one I can see huge potential in. Doesn't that deserve equal weight in the decision?"

"No, it does not."

"Why?"

"Because developing yet another covert ops training program in post-wartime does not carry the same prestige as DEVGRU. Nor will it strategically position you for your next lateral move." The Admiral studied his grandson's face, and seeing the anger Mitch wasn't trying to hide, shook his head. "I've proudly guided and supported your career since before its inception. But if you now choose to ignore my advice, I can only assume it means you no longer want my support."

With that the Admiral got to his feet and walked out.

Leaving Mitch with a ball of anger in his gut and a taste of bitterness in his mouth. And, of course, the bill.

11

BARELY A MONTH after her conversation with Tessa, Livi found out exactly how bad it could be when Pauline pushed the limits.

She'd been putting off the meeting since she'd returned from the cruise, but Pauline had insisted they needed to talk. Livi parked in the driveway in front of her mother's elegant townhouse just as her cell phone rang. Trying to shake off the exhaustion she'd been dragging around lately, Livi glanced at the display. And just like that, her fatigue, her worries, everything faded.

"If it isn't Super SEAL," she greeted, putting the call through her car's Bluetooth speakers so she could touch up her makeup before meeting her mom. "Are you in California?"

Every time they'd spoken over the last month he'd been somewhere else. Since he hadn't said where, Livi knew it wasn't one of the naval bases. The idea of him being off on a mission was a little worrisome, but she told herself she could handle it.

"I'll be en route soon."

"I can't wait." Livi smiled, angling her mirror as she slicked a fresh coat of Morning Taupe on her lips.

"I'm calling to check your availability for tomorrow," he said, his tone stiff and just a little formal. Still in military mode? Or with someone?

"Available for what, specifically?" Livi teased.

"I have a debt to pay," he reminded her. "I thought we could address that tomorrow evening."

A debt?

"Our date?" she remembered. "I'm pretty sure you paid that off."

"Negative. That payment was delayed," he reminded her, his words getting just a little lower. "We'll regroup and retry tomorrow, 1900 hours?"

Tomorrow was Valentine's Day. It was all Livi could do not to do a happy dance right there in the car.

"Will you be in uniform?" she asked in a husky voice. She got so turned on thinking about him in uniform. Even more so thinking of stripping him out of uniform.

"No."

Livi hesitated. It was just one word, a simple answer. Why did she feel he was angry?

"That's okay. I can imagine you in it." She paused before adding, "I'll be in nothing but my red stilettos."

The silence was electric. Livi pressed the tip of her tongue to her upper lip to keep from laughing as she imagined him in some barracks somewhere, surrounded by tough guys while he tried not to react.

"That's fine."

Fine?

Livi frowned. Usually he flirted back, playing word games using their own little sex code. It wasn't a very complex code. She was sure any SEAL—or Boy Scout—could break it. But it'd been fun.

"Will you be on the west coast for long?" She didn't want to make a big deal of it, but she'd so love to spend more time with him. She'd love even more to know he wanted to do the same.

"You know I can't divulge that." He didn't snap or sound aggressive. He simply stated the words in a flat tone that sent chills down her spine.

He must have been in an official setting. Or maybe just

coming off a major mission and still in the fighter mind-set. At least, that's what she told herself.

But she couldn't resist asking, "Is everything okay?"

"Fine." A second later, he repeated in a softer tone, "Fine."

It wasn't. Livi was sure it wasn't, but she knew better than to push. Glad she wasn't the issue, but wishing she could comfort, she did the only thing she could. Offer him a distraction.

"Be sure to bring your appetite," she told him. "I'm adding a little whipped cream to tomorrow night's ensemble."

Mitch cleared his throat. "Make that 1800."

She was still frowning when the line went dead.

Before she angled it back in place, she glanced at her reflection in the mirror. Despite the worry, she looked happy. A little pale, since she was still fighting some sort of tummy bug that she'd picked up a week ago, but her eyes were bright and her skin practically glowed.

Happy was a good look on her.

And she was getting really good at this, she decided as she slid from her car. She learned that not knowing things didn't bother her, and that even with most of the details of his day-to-day off conversational limits, they still had plenty to talk about. She missed seeing him, of course, but the phone calls a couple of times a week, the naughty video chats, kept the distance in check. She could definitely see herself doing this for quite a while, Livi realized. Because it felt good. It felt right.

It felt so good that maybe, soon, she'd even tell people about the two of them. Or maybe she'd keep him to herself for just a little longer.

Laughing, Livi let herself into her mom's place and called out a greeting. But her giddy delight didn't make it past the iced tea and crudités her mother had laid out.

"You did what?" she asked, having to force the hoarse words through the knot in her throat.

"I pulled in a few favors and arranged for you to shoot your Sexy SEAL Bodies fitness video on the Navy base in Coronado with an actual team of SEALs," Pauline said, her words ringing with triumph. She leaned forward in her leather chair, the chrome accents glinting as she gave Livi's knee a tap. "You'll begin shooting the third week of February."

"The third…" Livi pressed the tips of her fingers against her temple, hoping the pressure would ease the shooting pain. "Mother, that's next week."

"Time is of the essence, of course. We lost a lot of momentum with the holidays and the cruise. But we'll make up for it now. Or rather, starting tomorrow, since I've arranged a little dinner for all of the parties involved."

"I have plans tomorrow," Livi protested in a choked voice.

"You can change them, darling." Waving away Livi's red stilettos and whipped-cream dreams, Pauline bounded to her feet.

Apparently too excited to sit still, she started reeling off the myriad promotions, marketing angles and opportunities she'd lined up as she paced her living room.

Black leather, chrome and glass all played a quiet backdrop to the virulently loud art scattered around the space. Crimson and orange slashed across a canvas on one wall while twisting metal seemed to be rising from the ground across the room, ready to grab unsuspecting guests. Add Pauline's turquoise dress—and her bombshell news—to the mix and it made Livi feel ill.

"Isn't it fabulous? I've never had a deal come together this quickly. All I had to do was mention that Trent Evans had died trying to be a SEAL, and suddenly the gentleman in the Public Affairs office was ready to bend over backward to make this happen for us." Pauline rolled her eyes. "I think he's planning to build a campaign of his own out of the idea of giving back to one of their own."

Stunned, sure her mouth was hanging open, Livi could only shake her head. It took a lot of effort to find her voice, even more to keep from swearing when she did.

"Let me get this straight." She cleared her throat of all the cussing going on in her head. "All of my life, you refused to talk about, provide information or even acknowledge my father. Now you're suddenly ready to throw him on the altar as a sacrifice to the Gods of Getting Ahead?"

Pauline smoothed a hand over her hair, checking to be sure it was all tidy in its low ponytail as she considered the question.

Then she gave a sharp nod.

"If they'll have him, yes. Light the sacrificial flames. He might as well do something to finally contribute to your life, don't you think? And his name made a difference with that captain. The man pulled a few strings, put me in touch with a few connections, and voilà." Pauline waved her hand in the air with a snap. "We're good to go."

"No," Livi corrected, biting the word off with a snap of her teeth. "*We* are not good to go. *We* are not ready to begin. Without even getting into the moral issues that your methods bring up, there are plenty of other reasons this isn't ready to go."

No longer flitting around her room, Pauline stood in front of her daughter with an assessing expression on her face. Livi didn't know what she was looking for, or what she saw. And for once, she didn't care. This entire conversation was making her ill. She wanted it over with.

"I've barely written my adaption of the program. I haven't had time to work through the exercises on anything but paper, nor have I written the script. I don't have a workout crew, and even if I did, next week is too soon for them to know the program, too."

There were other reasons, of course. But after Pauline's reaction to Livi's comments about using Trent, Livi figured she'd keep her personal reasons to herself. Instead she arched her brow, hoping against hope that logic and reason would prevail. Experience, and the clawing nausea in her stomach, warned her otherwise.

"What's to write? The SEAL program is already written." Offering Livi a stiff smile, Pauline sat down again and did what she always did…focused on the situation at hand. No need to bring pesky things like emotions into the fray. "Their workout is famous, Olivia. Why would it need to be adapted?"

"Why?" Livi bit her lip, knowing a tantrum wouldn't help the situation. But man, she wished she could throw one, anyway. "A high school drama teacher doesn't hit the set, challenging Johnny Depp for the role of Jack Sparrow. A piano instructor wouldn't shove her way into Beethoven's house, plop down at his piano and charge people to listen to her play his symphony."

"Isn't Johnny Depp finished with that role? And correct me if I'm wrong, but Beethoven is dead." Pauline waited a beat, probably to give Livi time to finish grinding her teeth, then leaned forward to pat her daughter's knee. "Don't sell yourself short, darling. You're quite well-known in your own right. Your influence rating is even on par with some professional athletes, and you know all there is to know about exercise and fitness. This is the next logical step. You'll be famous."

But she didn't want to be famous.

As if an inky black wave had engulfed her, everything went dark and Livi felt the room spin. She gulped air, trying to level out her system. Passing out wouldn't convince Pauline of anything. But something had to.

Because the only thing Livi wanted to avoid more than fame was ruining what she had with Mitch. And her mother's latest scheme definitely wouldn't go over well. She'd seen how protective he was of the actual SEAL workout. And how unenthusiastic he'd been about her making another program based on it. He'd basically told her to stay out of his career not ten minutes ago. She was pretty sure this project would fly in the face of that request.

Still, thinking of Mitch calmed Livi. He was the most confident, self-assured person she'd ever met. How would he handle this? He'd tell her to take charge and put her wants and needs first. Ready to see how that felt, Livi took a deep breath. Once her emotions settled down, she offered her most composed, let's-be-reasonable smile.

"You should have discussed this with me, Mother."

"I'm discussing it with you now, aren't I?"

"After the fact."

"Of course. If I'd told you what I was planning, you'd have worked yourself into a nervous frenzy. This way you don't have time to be concerned."

"Right. So cutting me out of negotiations and keeping this project hush-hush until it was a done deal was, what? For my own good?" Forgetting being composed and reasonable, Livi crossed her arms over her chest, tapping one booted foot against the glossy ebony floor as she gave her mother a challenging stare. "You did an end run around me, making decisions you knew I'd be unhappy with."

Unable to tell a direct lie, Pauline took a deep breath of her own this time, sucking the air through pinched nostrils because her lips were clamped shut.

Livi grimaced. She should get up and walk out before her mother managed to unclamp her mouth. But suddenly there was more at stake than just this video arrangement— although that was enough on its own. She was sick and tired of trying to make everyone else happy at the expense of her own comfort.

Livi's fists were clenched as much against the surge of anger in her gut as against the nausea.

It had to end.

"I didn't agree to film on base or with the actual SEALs. I don't want to do this format or take the workout in this direction," she stated. Even as part of her cried out against everything that'd mean giving up, and another part freaked at the idea of letting people down, Livi set her chin. "I want out of this deal."

"And how do you propose to get out of it?" Pauline asked, her words so cold they might as well have dripped icicles.

"I don't care how you do it," Livi dismissed. "That's for you to deal with."

"For me to…" Looking as if her daughter had just told her she was quitting her job to be a kitten skinner, Pauline's face froze in shock before turning pale white. It only took a second, though, for anger to stain her cheeks red. "So once again, you want no input in the running of your own business except to complain? That's not how this works, Olivia."

Livi knew she'd ignored a lot of the elements of running Stripped Down Fitness, but damn it, that didn't mean it wasn't still her company. Pauline worked for her. Not the other way around.

"I'm tired of how things used to work. I'm tired of other people running my life. First Derrick, now you. It has to end."

"If you're unhappy with my management, that's fine. We can end it," Pauline snapped. "But first I'm going to remind you of a couple of things."

"Oh, you are, are you?" Livi rolled her eyes, feeling as if she'd degenerated into a mouthy teenager with braces on her teeth. She knew she was being obnoxious. She didn't even know why, since this sort of behavior wouldn't get her anywhere with her mother. All it'd do was make the situation worse. If she wanted to get through to Pauline, she had to be reasonable, logical.

She knew all of that.

But she simply couldn't make herself care.

"Is this where you tell me how you saved me and my career? This is the part where you take credit for my success and point out all of the ways I should be thanking you?" Gee, didn't that sound familiar.

Pauline goggled.

That was the only possible way to describe her slack-jawed, wide-eyed look of absolute shock.

"Olivia Kane, what has gotten into you?" she snapped as soon as she recovered enough to make her jaw work again. "I will not tolerate being spoken to like that."

"Okay." Feeling sick to her stomach, at herself, at the entire situation, Livi surged to her feet.

Whoa. She wiped her hand over her damp forehead and, ignoring the little black dots dancing in front of her eyes, grabbed her purse.

One step and she knew she was in trouble.

"Olivia, I'm not finished. Where do you think you're going?"

Livi didn't slow her sprint, but she did yell over her shoulder as she hurried toward her mother's stainless steel bathroom.

"To throw up."

MITCH HAD NEVER considered himself to be a romantic guy, and he was pretty sure the last Valentine's Day he'd celebrated had included construction paper and paste.

But he thought he'd done pretty well tonight. He glanced around the posh, candlelit cabin and nodded. He'd rented a private yacht for their romantic moonlit cruise for two on the San Diego Bay that included a gourmet dinner, a vase of roses and a box of chocolates. Yeah, he thought he'd pulled it off nicely.

And the expression on Livi's face told him she agreed.

"This is all so beautiful," she murmured, looking out the cabin window at the ocean.

"You're beautiful," he said, looking across the small table at her. The tiny red dress did amazing things to the view, but it was her face that held his attention. She actually seemed to glow in the candlelight.

"There's something I wanted to tell you that happened with my video schedule," she said, the words coming in a rush, as if she were trying to force them out as fast as she could.

"No—" he interrupted. The irritating memory of his grandfather's recent advice still causing his guts to clench, Mitch shook his head. "No business tonight. No career talk. Just us."

Livi's lips parted, her eyes wide and just a little nervous. Then she nodded. "Okay. No business. But if we don't include any talk about our careers, what's left?"

Mitch took one of her hands in his, raising her slender fingers to his mouth. Brushing his lips over her knuckles, he challenged, "Let's find out."

Two hours later, what he'd found out worried him just a little. Their common ground was vast, their differences interesting.

Her hand still wrapped in his, Mitch led Livi along the ship's deck to stand at the aft railing, where they could watch the moonlight together.

"It's so lovely," she breathed, snugging against him.

"You're cold," he realized aloud when he felt her shiver. Looking around, he saw the blanket he'd requested on a nearby bench, grabbed it and wrapped it around her. "Here, this should help."

"Mmm," she murmured, pulling the soft cashmere close then curling up against him again. "You've thought of everything."

For a few moments, they stared out at the moon, both appreciating the view of it glistening on the waves. Mitch felt Livi's barely smothered yawn and glanced down.

"Bored?"

"No, sorry," she said with an embarrassed laugh. "This is an absolutely wonderful evening. I've just been tired lately."

She'd been looking pale in the morning, too, he remembered. And the few times he'd spoken with her before he'd returned to Southern California she'd sounded pretty drained.

"You're working too hard," he observed with a frown. "You've seemed worn-out ever since that cruise."

"Just having trouble refilling the energetic well, I think," she said. "I don't do well being 'on' for such an extended period of time. Even when I did the Fit To Be Naked tour, I had a lot of quiet time, me time. But on a cruise ship, that's not possible. I knew going in that it'd be draining, but I didn't realize just how draining."

Mitch scowled at the water.

He didn't want tonight to be about their careers because he didn't want to think about his. Especially about the choices ahead of him. If he chose DEVGRU, Mitch knew it'd essentially be the end of their relationship. He'd be stationed in Virginia, undergoing intensive training. There was no way they could make a relationship work with that sort of distance, with the intense demands on his time, energy, life.

Still, he felt compelled to protect her. Pulling Livi around so her back was snuggled to his front, he wrapped his arms around her waist and surrounded her with warmth.

Then he did the same with his carefully worded advice.

"Perhaps you could integrate more leisure into your

schedule," he suggested. "Reconsider accepting projects that stress you out and focus on the ones you feel the best about."

"In other words, don't work so hard, stand up to my manager about scheduling and don't do anything I don't want?" she clarified with a laugh. Turning, Livi looped her hands around the back of his neck and gave Mitch a chiding smile. "I thought we weren't talking career stuff."

"Okay, just a little career stuff." He brushed his lips over hers. "I want you to be happy. I'm coming to realize how important that is to me."

Livi's eyes widened, emotions filling them so deeply Mitch felt as if he could drown in the power of them.

"I am happy," she said. Then she smiled as if it were a new discovery. "I really am. I'm in a wonderful position to do something I love. I have a message to share with people and a great platform to do it from. I have a relationship with an incredible man who makes me even happier."

Seeing the declaration in her eyes, just there on the tip of her tongue ready to be shared, Mitch did something he'd never done before in his life. He panicked. He couldn't hear those words yet. Not when he didn't know if he could respond with his heart, or with his mind.

So he sidestepped.

"You're an amazing woman," he told her, his fingers skimming through the hair tangling around her. "You've built an incredible business in a highly competitive market. That takes smart strategy, sure, but it also takes something special."

"Maybe. I know it's always interesting, if nothing else," she said with a small shrug, her gaze still bright but a little shuttered, as if she'd pulled those huge emotions back behind a safety barrier. "I face challenges, of course. But that's a good thing, right? What's life without those?"

"You mean challenges like overcoming your shyness?"

"More like deciding on the right direction to go in next," she said quietly. The wind danced around them, rocking the boat and blowing through Livi's hair. "I feel as if I'm at a crossroad. One path is familiar, and while it's not always comfortable, at least I know it's a secure, well-thought-out path."

Frowning a little, Mitch tucked a swath of her silky hair so he could more clearly see her face. It sounded as if they were on the same path, both facing the same choices. Different terrains and directions, of course. But still…

"What's on the other path?" he asked.

"I don't know." She gave a delighted laugh. "That's so tempting and scary and intriguing, isn't it? But it could also be a huge mistake. I'm always afraid to make those."

Yeah. Him, too.

"Which path do you want to take?" Which did he want to take?

"The one that makes me happy, I suppose. It's hard to know which that is, though, isn't it?"

"What would make you happiest?" he asked quietly.

"For someone to love me," she said, her smile so beautiful it made his heart ache. "To be loved and understood and accepted. Not a huge dream, but it's my biggest."

Mitch cupped her face in his hands, lifting it to his. He stared deep into her eyes, wishing so much that he could make her dream come true. Her smile shook a little, either at the intensity of his gaze or at what she saw in his own eyes.

As much in caution against what she might be seeing as in desperate need, Mitch took her mouth.

There were a thousand words in his kiss.

Passionate words, needy words. Persuasively tempting words. He put everything he couldn't say into that kiss. Everything he wanted, everything he hoped for—even dreams he'd never realized he had until her.

But even as he pulled her onto the deck chair and wrapped himself around her, letting the kiss take them deeper, Mitch was careful.

He'd put all of those words and emotions in that kiss.

But he didn't give the one thing he didn't think he could offer.

A promise.

12

MITCH CROSSED THE COMPOUND, his shoulders stiffening when he noticed the looks heading his way. He'd been getting them all day.

Actually, he'd gotten looks all his life. A man dedicated to perfecting his career, to knowing just what to train in, where to be at what time in order to accelerate his ascent up the ranks got a lot of stares. When that man was the son of a captain, with a grandfather like Admiral Donovan, speculation always came with the stares.

Mitch had faced jealousy, accusations of nepotism and even hate because of his success.

But these stares were different.

Mocking. Angry. Derisive, even.

What the hell was going on? He'd been off base on leave since Valentine's Day, staying at Livi's instead of hitting the barracks. You'd think if something ugly had gone down somebody would have contacted him.

He strode through the building toward Captain Goodman's office, wondering if whatever was going down was the reason the AOIC of the SEALs had summoned him. He knew how to read the signs. Nobody had the battle vibe, but there was no worry in the air. Whatever was being aimed his way, it was personal.

Had his CSAR slipup become public knowledge? Was a minor distraction enough to merit the kind of hostility being directed toward him?

When he walked into Goodman's office, though, the

reason for the summons, at least, became clear. Anger replaced confusion in Mitch's gut as he stood at attention.

"Donovan," the captain greeted. "You know Captain Tilden?"

Sure, he remembered the Public Affairs asshole who'd gleefully handed him the *fluff* SEAL-workout assignment.

Mitch nodded, barely giving Tilden a glance.

"The captain has instructed me that your team will be taking part in a promotional venture that will benefit the Navy and highlight the SEALs," Goodman said, his tone as neutral as the beige walls behind him. "Your team will participate in the filming of a fitness video featuring the SEAL workout."

Shock rocked through his system so hard it left a ringing in his ears and a vicious gnawing in his gut.

"This is good publicity. It'll bring in recruits, enhance the image of the SEALs' manliness and make the Navy look good," Tilden said in that aww-shucks voice. "You boys will get to be movie stars. Or video stars, at least. Can't say that happens every day."

Neither did breaking a superior officer into a dozen tiny pieces and pulverizing them to dust. Mitch ground his teeth together to bite back his initial response. Once he was sure he had a handle on it, he looked at Goodman.

"Permission to speak freely, sir?"

Goodman leaned back in his chair, slanted a look of dislike toward Tilden and nodded.

"Go ahead."

"With all due respect to the Captain's concerns about our public image, the SEALs don't need a promotional campaign, nor do we need publicity. Elements of our training, such as BUD/S, have been documented before. Unlike programs such as that, this…" What did he call it? Ridiculous idea? Idiotic proposal? Clusterfuck from hell? "This is a commercial venture that would be profiting from the

SEALs. Our involvement would provide tacit approval of whatever the final project became, over which we'd have no control. I strongly advise against it."

"But I'm not asking for advice," Tilden said, his good ol' boy facade falling away. His beady eyes glittered with dislike. "I'm ordering you to report for filming Monday morning at oh-seven-hundred with a fully briefed eight-man team."

Tilden paused for a moment before leaning forward in his seat with a toothy smile and adding, "Tell them to smile pretty for the cameras."

Mitch eyed the jackass in front of him.

He'd never hated a superior officer before. He wasn't even sure he'd actually hated another person before.

He did now.

"The orders come from Rear Admiral Morse," Goodman said quietly. "I've confirmed it."

Mitch's jaw clenched. But not nearly as tightly as his gut.

"Permission to be excused."

"Well, now—" His fat hand on a thick file, Tilden obviously wanted to keep playing.

"Permission granted," Goodman interrupted, pulling the file out and handing it to Mitch with a nod.

He felt a vicious sense of satisfaction turning his back on Tilden before the man could say another word.

The file fisted against his side, Mitch refused to look at it until he was clear of the building and halfway across the base. Not because he was worried about turning around and beating Tilden's tiny pinhead against the wall.

But because he knew what was inside. He was sure he knew who had instigated this humiliating little jaunt. He'd kissed her goodbye not more than four hours ago.

Focus, he reminded himself when his anger intensified. *Contain and diffuse first.*

With that in mind, he was determined to handle the situation before any of the SEAL teams returned from maneuvers that afternoon. He hadn't counted on the support crew, the bevy of non-SEAL personnel who served with the team.

He was hit with a dozen furious faces when he stepped into the team headquarters.

"What's the deal, Donovan?"

"Rumor says you got your girlfriend a sweet job using the SEALs."

"Must be nice, using connections for everything," someone else muttered from the back of the crowd.

Fury was a new feeling for Mitch. He was a man used to respect. He had spent his life courting it, counting on it.

He'd never faced a lack of it, and for a brief moment, he wasn't sure how to react. Beating the hell out of the men seemed a little extreme. So he did the only thing he could do. He listened to them with the same respect he expected in return.

Mitch waited, but the complaints didn't wind down. So he stopped them by simply raising his hand.

"The video is happening. A crew will be here filming Monday," he told them. "Orders for this project are coming from the Public Affairs office. I've already requested a meeting with the base commander, and for someone from JAG to prohibit any on-camera involvement of the SEALs," he said quietly. And then, because there was nothing left to add that would change the men's opinion of him, Mitch did an about-face and walked out.

It took three hours before he felt confident that he'd diffused the situation to his and the team's satisfaction.

What he hadn't—couldn't—change was the fact that there would be a fitness video based on the Navy SEAL workout filmed here, at the Navy SEAL training center, and that he'd been pulled from the covert-ops program to oversee it.

Or that the woman he'd been thinking he loved enough

to reconsider his career path had screwed over that very career.

It took two phone calls and the promise of an as-yet-unnamed favor for Mitch to track Livi down.

Checking the address against his note, he confirmed that the cement building was the one he was looking for. It wasn't until he reached the entrance that he saw the simple sign stamped in block letters over the doors.

Stripped Down Fitness.

Did she run her business out of here?

Curiosity running a dim second to anger, Mitch shoved open the doors and marched inside. And stopped short.

It was a gym.

But not the kind he'd have expected to find Livi in.

He'd watched her videos. Not just the stripper ones, although those had been worth a second and third viewing. But her various other videos, as well. The settings in them were all sleek, clean—simple lines and bright colors. It all coordinated, right down to the clothes the people exercising with her wore.

But this place… Well, he supposed it color-coordinated.

The cement walls were the same steel gray as the outside, cracks showing here and there behind the mirrored expanse. There were black padded mats beneath all of the equipment and in the various workout areas, but the paths between were again cement.

The machines were top-of-the-line, many of them the same as were in the Navy's gym. The weights were metal, not a Popsicle-hued one in sight. Bright lighting and the buzz of conversation finished the mise-en-scène of a serious gym for serious workouts.

For a fitness diva, Livi sure didn't seem to understand the idea of posh and plush. Which was probably the point, he realized. This place was stripped of all but the necessities. It had one purpose and one purpose only.

Fitness.

Just like her videos.

Mitch's jaw worked as irritation surged again at the reminder of why he was here.

And just where was The Body Babe?

His eyes found her immediately halfway across the crowded gym.

Dressed in bright red shorts, a black-and-red exercise bra and tennis shoes, she stood by one of the workout benches.

At first he thought she was coaching the mountain of a bodybuilder as she gestured to the barbell.

Then she stepped up to the black metal rod, her shoulders loose, her eyes focused. She huffed out a breath, wrapped her hands around the bar and lifted.

Mitch's brow arched.

He was in excellent condition.

That wasn't ego, it was simple fact.

But, damn… Olivia Kane's body was even tighter than his.

His abs were cut. But Livi's six-pack was rock solid.

His body was a weapon. Hers was an homage to fitness.

But her homage was screwing with the comfort of his weapon. And that couldn't be tolerated.

Mitch strode over and waited, arms crossed over his chest while she curled the barbell. Despite his irritation, he couldn't help but be impressed. Her form was perfect, from the slight bend in her knees to the angle of her shoulders. Chin high, her focus was anchored somewhere in front of her as she breathed with her lifts.

Her body glistened.

It wasn't until she put the barbell back on its stand that he saw her grimace. She pressed one hand to her stomach and closed her eyes for a second.

"You okay, Liv?" the bodybuilder asked gruffly.

"Just a little light-headed, Bo," she said. "I probably didn't eat enough protein with lunch."

"You were feeling bad yesterday, too," Mitch interrupted without thinking. "Maybe you should see a doctor."

Two sets of eyes turned his way. The bodybuilder's filled with suspicion, Livi's with delight. Despite her welcoming smile, she was pale. Despite her glistening muscles, she looked fragile.

And despite his bone-deep anger, he wanted to pull her into his arms and protect her.

But he wished like hell he didn't.

"Can we talk?"

USUALLY SHE WAS thrilled to see Mitch. But given that he looked as if he could bite the bumper-plate weight off her barbell and spit it out as bullets, Livi didn't need to hear ominous words to clue in that something was wrong.

Pulse jumping, her stomach pitched into her toes, and somewhere between the two, her already queasy stomach threatened to revolt.

"Sure," she said with her brightest show-no-fear smile. "I didn't expect to see you here."

She hadn't even known he had a clue where her business was. But then, he was Super SEAL, so she shouldn't have been surprised he'd found it.

"Seems as if everyone is getting something unexpected today, aren't they?" he observed coolly.

"I'm sorry?" Her smile dimmed.

"We need to talk," he said again. Glancing around, he added, "Privately."

"Fine." Her smile gone now, she gave him a searching look. "My office is right over there."

"Aren't you the businesswoman," he observed, tilting his head to indicate that she lead the way.

Bo, obviously not liking Mitch's tone, gave a low growl.

"It's okay," she murmured, giving Bo a reassuring smile. The big man's scowl didn't change, but he finally nodded and stepped aside.

Mitch didn't say a word. He didn't even seem to care that a three-time IWF champion was poised to use him to do an overhead press. Then again, Mitch was almost superhuman. He had no reason to care about something like that.

What was he worried about, though? Livi snagged a clean towel off the linen shelf on her way across the gym, dabbing at the beads of sweat on her chest.

As soon as they reached her office, she turned to tell Mitch that she did, indeed, have a doctor's appointment the next morning. But before she could say a word, he slapped the door shut and assumed a combative stance. Legs wide, arms crossed over his chest.

Livi took a step back, her butt hitting the desk and almost knocking her off her feet.

"What's going on?" she asked with a frown. Everything had been wonderful the previous night. No matter how much she'd warned herself to live in the moment and not buy into happy-ever-after, she was starting to believe in *happy for a really long time* with Mitch.

At least, she had been starting to believe.

"Were you involved in the Navy SEAL video deal that would have you filming a workout program on my base, with my men, using my fitness program?"

"I tried to mention that last night, but you said you didn't want to discuss business," Livi reminded him, starting to get irritated.

Before Livi could ask why it was an issue, Mitch strode forward until he was chest to chest with her. Which wasn't nearly as sexy as it had always been in the past.

"You admit that you knew about the video."

"Obviously." Livi gave him a baffled look. Why was he acting so obnoxious? "So did you. If you recall, you're the one who walked me through your gym, gave me a copy of an official—if obsolete—SEAL workout and listened to my ideas for the video I'd be filming."

"But that's not how the deal ended up, is it?"

Bristling at the sarcasm in his voice, Livi lifted her hands in askance.

"I know my mother discussed expanding the video to have a much more SEAL-focused presentation, but I preferred to stay with the original format," Livi said carefully.

Had Pauline not cancelled filming? The only contact Livi had had with her since the vomiting incident was a text stating she'd instructed their attorney to adjust the contract as per Livi's orders and would advise accordingly.

She opened her mouth to tell Mitch the whole story.

"Your manager is actually your mother?" he said before she got her first word out.

Why did he keep interrupting her?

"So?" Frustrated, Livi pulled the hairband out so she could shove her fingers through her loosened hair to try and relieve some of the building tension.

"This would be the same mother who was abandoned by your father in his attempt to become a SEAL. The same mother who hates all military men and of whom you said would have a fit if she knew about us."

Why was he picking on her mother? Irritation overtaking confusion, anger starting to drown out hurt, Livi shifted to her full height and met his hard look with one of her own.

"I don't know what you want me to say," she admitted. "I'm not denying my parental issues. But I don't see why you have a problem with them."

"The problem is that one way or another, you, your mother or both went behind my back and used the information you gleaned from spending time with me to manipulate your way into a deal with the Navy to make a fitness video!"

If he'd punched her in the belly, Livi couldn't have been more hurt. Trying to breathe through the shocking pain of his words, she could only shake her head.

"You believe that of me? That I would lie to you, manipulate our relationship, use you for my own profit?"

Mitch didn't say a word. But his silence spoke volumes. And Livi heard every decibel.

She gave up standing up to him toe to toe because her knees simply wouldn't support her. Instead, she sank onto her desk, holding it with both hands against the wave of dizzy horror. Not just at his words, but at the ugly message beneath them.

"I was told that filming begins next Monday. Filming with your company." He waited a beat. "Tell me, are you bringing strippers for backup or are you going to ask the SEAL team to bump and grind?"

Livi waited for the room to stop spinning and took a deep breath. Then another.

But none of that changed what she was hearing.

Still, hoping she was wrong, she clarified, "Are you angry because of the workout video itself? Or are you angry because the workout video is with me, in particular?"

Despite the buzzing in her ears, she forced herself to focus on Mitch's face. Looking into his eyes—the eyes she'd fallen in love with—she didn't need to hear his answer. Because it was right there.

"Do you have any idea the damage you've caused with this?" he sidestepped. "How this association has lost me the respect of half the support staff, and most likely my own SEAL team."

Right. Respect.

Promising herself she could fall into a puddle of misery as soon as this was over, Livi pulled herself together, stood on her feet and faced her heartbreak head-on.

"The issue isn't so much that you feel I manipulated you

by luring you into my bed in order to connive the US Navy into boosting my career. The issue is that you're a snob."

"The hell I am."

"The problem isn't that you didn't know about the video, because we both know that you did," she continued hoarsely. Livi cleared her throat, refusing to give in to the pain. "But because somehow, an association with me is humiliating to your reputation. You're being razzed by your buddies, judged by your peers. Suddenly everything else you've done doesn't matter because this one single thing puts an ugly spotlight on you. And you don't like it."

"Would you?"

"No, actually I don't like it at all. It's always been the crux of my issue with performing in public. But I had no idea how much worse it would be when it came from someone I—" She broke off and took a breath before finishing. "By someone I cared about. Someone who should know better."

Despite her best intentions, Livi's eyes welled up and her lower lip trembled. She bit into it.

"Don't cry," he ordered.

"Oh, don't worry," she told him after taking a very worrisome, shaky breath. "I'm not about to put you in the position of having to overcome your distaste for my feelings."

"That's not what I'd said, nor what I'd meant." Mitch scowled. "You're twisting my words."

"And you twisted actions I didn't make into an attack on your career."

His scowl deepened, but he didn't bother denying it.

"You've told me to stop putting other people's wants ahead of my own feelings. Well, I'm taking your advice." She swallowed hard, hurting like she'd never imagined she could. Then she pointed to the door. "I want you to leave. I won't discuss this right now, and I don't want to hear anything else you have to say."

"This can't be resolved without discussion," he pointed out.

"What's to resolve?" she wondered through the pain. Terrified she'd humiliate herself, Livi drew on strength she hadn't realized she had as she stepped around Mitch to open the door.

She waited, hanging on to the doorknob as if it were a lifeline.

Frowning, Mitch looked as if he wasn't sure if he wanted to argue or check her temperature.

Since that was even more humiliating, Livi said, "Please. I'd like you to go."

"I'll give you a call," he told her before walking out without a backward glance.

Why? He'd already broken her heart.

And then she burst into tears.

"PREGNANT?" SHOCK MINGLING with the pain of the impossible, Livi shook her head. "I can't be."

"To have a nickel for every time I've heard that," Dr. Heath said, her eyes dancing behind round glasses. "The tests are conclusive, Olivia. You're definitely pregnant."

"But I have PCOS. You said the odds of my conceiving were virtually nonexistent." She tried to think, but the buzzing was so loud in her ears. "We used a condom."

"The odds of conceiving with Polycystic Ovarian Syndrome are slim, and the odds of protection against pregnancy with a condom are high." Dr. Heath paused and then gave Livi a bright smile. "There's a reason they call this a miracle, though. Sometimes, the odds simply don't matter."

Somehow, Livi got through the rest of her appointment.

Then she did what any girl would do when faced with this kind of news. The only thing she could do.

She went to see her mother.

"Olivia," Pauline greeted coolly when her secretary quietly shut the door behind them. "I told you the attorneys were handling the SEAL workout. Are you here to complain about something else?"

"No," Livi said faintly, crossing the plush gold carpet to sink into one of the wide chairs in front of her mother's antique desk. Pauline's home was modern and edgy. But with its purples, golds, antiques and leather, her office was fit for a queen. "I spoke with the attorney this morning. They've assured me we're under no obligation. Actually the Navy isn't happy with the agreement, either, so there will be no issue cancelling the contract. Everything is fine."

"Fine?" Pauline tapped her nails against her desk for a moment. "Well, I'm glad ending your chances at a lucrative deal turned out fine, then."

Her back automatically going up at her mother's disdainful tone, Livi was about to point out that the Navy had nixed the deal, too. Then she stopped. She wasn't here to argue. And, she realized, her mother was right. It would have been a lucrative deal. Just like all of the ones Pauline had pulled together. Because no matter what else could be said, Pauline had always put Livi first.

"Mother, I'm grateful for everything you've done over the last couple of years for Stripped Down Fitness. You put aside so much to save this company, and my reputation. I really do appreciate it," Livi told her sincerely, glad her voice didn't shake.

"You made your feelings about my management perfectly clear last week," Pauline reminded her with a chilly arch of her brow. "Is this the follow-up where you ask me to step down?"

Like she did before lifting a heavy weight, Livi puffed out a breath, braced herself and mentally stepped up.

"My behavior last week was petty and childish," Livi

admitted. "I was upset about the SEAL video because I thought Mitch would be angry. I didn't admit that, though, because I was trying to hide my relationship with him from you."

From the look on her mother's face, she'd been silly to think she'd hidden anything.

"You said those were your reasons last week," Pauline reminded her in a tone that suggested Livi better hurry up.

"Right." Another deep breath. Livi opened her mouth. No words came out, so she tried again. "I'm pregnant."

Livi steeled herself for the slew of recriminations, "I told you so"s and well-deserved anger. She met her mother's gaze without flinching.

"I beg your pardon?"

In complete empathy with that stunned reaction, Livi repeated, "I'm pregnant, Mother. The doctor just confirmed it."

And watched Pauline's brown eyes—so like her own—fill with tears.

"Please, no," Livi begged as she jumped to her feet. "I thought you'd yell at or lecture me. Don't cry."

"I'm sorry." Pauline waved her fingers under her eyes to dry them, then took a deep breath and offered a shaky smile. "It's just…well, my little girl is having a baby? It's emotional."

"And now someone will be calling you Grandmother," Livi said with a wet laugh.

"Oh." The tears slid over. Livi honestly wasn't sure if it was sentiment, or if Pauline was facing the idea that she was old enough to own that particular title. Either way, she rose and met her mom halfway for a hug.

She was shocked to feel her mother's fingers clutching her back in return, holding her close while Pauline buried her face in Livi's hair for a moment.

And then the older woman flipped the control switch back on.

"I thought you'd be angry," Livi admitted as her mother released her.

"Angry?" Pauline shot her an incredulous look as she moved to her desk to find tissues. "That would be rather hypocritical of me, wouldn't it?"

Livi blinked. She hadn't even thought of it that way.

"I thought you agreed with Derrick," she said quietly. "That I was better off without children, and that they'd get in the way of my career."

"I repeat, that'd be rather hypocritical of me, as I've built a wonderful career and raised a daughter while doing so." Looking as baffled as Livi felt, Pauline shook her head. "And please, why would you compare me to that man? He was an ass."

And she, apparently, was an idiot. Why had she never asked her mother about any of this before? Instead, she'd always been afraid to speak up, figuring her mother would shut her out as she had about her father. So she'd never tried.

"Did the doctor clear you to exercise?" Pauline asked, worry clear in her eyes. That Livi was pregnant was its own little miracle. They both knew staying so would be another one. "I can contact your clients, make other arrangements if necessary."

Livi swallowed hard to clear the tears from her throat and shook her head.

"The doctor gave me a list of precautions. I'll have to be careful. I can do personal training, but nothing as intensive as what I'm known for," she said. She puffed out a breath and once again laid her career at her mother's feet with the request for help. This time, though, it wasn't out of desperation. It was because she truly wanted her mother on her team. "What do I do? I can't pay my debts as well as support myself and a baby on just my income from the gym and my coaching fees."

"I'll call your accountant and attorney and set up a meeting for later this week," Pauline said. "We'll assess the situation, get their input and look at the various opportunities available."

"And in the meantime?" Livi wondered, feeling lost.

"In the meantime, you figure out what you want from your career," Pauline instructed, getting to her feet.

"How?" Overwhelmed by the idea, Livi shook her head. "I don't even know where to start."

"You look at what's profitable and what has potential. You weigh your options—benefits versus costs."

"Then what?"

"Then *you* decide," Pauline said.

Livi laughed at the extra emphasis on the "you," appreciating that despite the ugly way she'd complained, her mother had still listened.

"This time, consider everything you enjoy, everything you hate, as well," Pauline said. "Really think it through. If it's something that makes you miserable, it's not worth doing."

"Why didn't you suggest that before when I was unhappy?" Livi wondered.

"Because you never told me how you felt in such stridently specific terms before," Pauline pointed out.

Nope. She'd been too busy keeping her feelings to herself. Livi vowed then and there to never do that again. Whatever her feelings were, they were worthy of being shared. Even if the other person didn't want to hear them.

"Of course, even if you had, I was so focused on ensuring your security that I probably wouldn't have listened," her mother admitted.

Probably?

But how could she blame her mother for taking control when Livi had been so determined not to?

"Will you still manage me?" Livi asked softly.

Pauline gave her a long look then angled her head in a gesture of agreement.

"For now I want you to go home and take a nice, long nap," Pauline instructed. "Do you have dinner plans? Would you like me to bring something by?"

On cue, her phone signaled an incoming text. Livi glanced at the display, feeling numb when she saw it was from Mitch.

"Is everything okay?"

"I suppose." Livi puffed out a breath, then tucked her phone away. "Mitch wants to talk with me."

"You'll tell him about the baby."

Brows tight, Livi glanced up at her mother. She didn't want to tell him. If she'd thought he was furious with her for screwing up his career the other day, she couldn't even imagine how he'd react when she told him she'd screwed up his life, too.

"Olivia?" Pauline prompted in a stern tone.

"Does that mom voice come with childbirth?" Livi hoped, still a little giddy at the idea of actually becoming a mom and finding out.

"No. It comes from years of raising a child and knowing when she's considering doing something stupid."

"I'm going to tell him," Livi insisted. Then she pulled a face. "But couldn't I do it next week? Maybe after I've figured out the rest of my life?"

Weren't two huge, life-changing situations in a week enough?

"Will it make the next week any easier knowing you haven't told him?"

Her shoulders dropped like weights, taking Livi's stomach along with them. But she offered her mother a queasy smile.

"No. But it will make our breakup a lot more interesting."

13

Mitch sat nursing a beer in a hole-in-the-wall bar, his cell phone at his elbow, wondering when Livi would respond to his text. He'd told her he'd call. One way or another, they needed to resolve where they stood.

It'd been a whole day since he'd messaged her. He wanted to text again, but he figured it was better to wait until she was ready to talk. That'd give him time to solidify what he wanted.

The problem was, for the first time in his life he didn't have a clue what that'd be.

He knew what he should want. And he knew what he thought he wanted. But like the two paths Livi had so romantically painted on Valentine's Day, it was impossible to know which was right, which was real and which was just a pipe dream.

Her suggestion to end things was obviously the best choice. He'd already hurt her—why drag it out further? He should simply let it go, chalk it all up to great sex and a little fun. She was interfering with his career, whether she meant to or not.

And nothing, nobody, should be more important than his career.

Except he was miserable thinking about ending it like that. He hated the idea of his life without her. And he'd willingly offered up everything to his career. Blood, sweat, devotion and, on more than one occasion, his life.

But the Admiral was right. Livi was a distraction.

It'd be crazy to think that'd change. She wasn't the kind

of woman who'd ever fade into the background. So what did that mean? To be in a relationship he'd have to quit the Navy? Mitch frowned at the mocking black screen on his cell phone.

What was he if not a SEAL? If not a sailor? Were those two paths absolute? A or B? No mixing of the two?

When someone slid onto the stool next to him, Mitch didn't have to glance over to know who it was. He didn't even bother asking how he'd found him in a dingy bar off his usual beaten track. The old man had his ways.

Both men were silent as the bartender brought another beer. He glanced at Mitch, who shook his head.

The old man waited until the bartender had meandered back to the other end of the bar, then in a move he'd been making since Mitch had turned twenty-one, clinked his frosty bottle against his son's lukewarm one.

"I hear I've got a problem on my hands," Thomas said after a silent minute.

"I hear I'm about to be labeled TARFU," Mitch mused, his eyes locked on his beer as he tossed out the standard military jargon for *totally and royally fucked up*. "Guess you were called in to diffuse the situation?"

"Assess and advise."

Mitch grunted.

"Your mother thinks you've fallen in love," Thomas observed conversationally. "She's afraid your new woman will steal her baby boy away. She's got this silly notion this woman will take her place in your heart and take over your life before she's had a chance to give her the Denise Donovan seal of approval. That's what mothers do, I suppose."

"She sicced the Admiral on me," Mitch pointed out, not having a whole lot of sympathy for his mother's maternal drama. "Is that what mothers do? Stir up enough trouble that Grandfather took personal time, flew across the country and hauled me out of training in order to explain the error of my ways?"

His grandfather's disapproval still burned in Mitch's gut. And, he realized, he'd taken that anger out on Livi. How did that make him any better than the Admiral?

"You've got every right to fall in love with whomever you want, son. Just like you have the right to make your own career choices." Thomas shrugged. "That your granddaddy is getting his skivvies in a twist over them is his problem. Not yours."

Mitch sat with that image for a moment, letting it play through his mind. Then he turned and looked at his father for the first time since the older man had sat down next to him.

"His skivvies in a twist?" Mitch repeated incredulously.

Unabashed, Thomas laughed.

"It's something I heard your mother say. Actually her term was *panties*, but I can't say as I want that image in my head."

"Ditto that." Mitch gave a half laugh and shook his head. "You might not want to let the Admiral hear you say it either way, though."

Thomas took a long drink, set his bottle on the bar and offered a direct look at odds with his usually affable expression.

"I'm going to do something I've rarely done, son. I'm going to give you a piece of advice."

Mitch's brows drew together as he realized how true those words were. His grandfather had always been the one to offer up advice, solicited or otherwise. His mother had an opinion about everything and loved nothing more than to share her vision of her son's life. But Thomas? He answered questions, he offered his experiences, he disciplined and guided. But giving advice wasn't in his repertoire.

Curiosity overcoming his irritation about the entire situation, Mitch angled his body toward the old man. This could get interesting.

"The Admiral has played a big part in your life, all of your life. He's the head of the family and has strong feelings about that."

For the first time, Mitch wondered if that'd ever bothered Thomas. Before Mitch could ask, Thomas was speaking again.

"My father is a good man. He's strong, fair and dedicated to serving." Thomas took a swig of his beer and gave Mitch a long look, as if gauging whether his son could handle the information he was about to impart. "But he's also an elitist and a snob."

Mitch snorted, first in surprise, then again in agreement. No arguing with facts.

He waited a few seconds. Then he tilted his head toward Thomas and arched both brows.

"That's it?"

"That's it."

"Okay." Mitch gave a slow nod. "But I'm not sure that's actually advice."

"Sure it is. You just have to think about it." Thomas waited a beat and asked, "Why are you considering the DEVGRU assignment?"

"Why?" Mitch considered the question carefully. "It's an honor to serve on that level. If I were a part of DEVGRU I'd be at the pinnacle. I'd be a part of the most elite force in the world."

"All compelling reasons," Thomas observed. "It's a move that would definitely cement your reputation, garner you numerous accolades and most definitely quiet the whispers that you got where you are based on nepotism."

Mitch frowned. Why did those sound like bad things when his father said them?

"Livi called me a snob," he admitted.

His face carefully blank, Thomas simply drank his beer and shrugged.

"You're a lot like your grandfather, son."

Mitch had heard that his entire life. He'd always taken pride in that, had actually pushed himself to be more like the Admiral in order to garner more of just that sort of observation.

But now... Mitch figured if he had a choice, he'd rather be like his father. His reputation might not get as many awed comments, but his life would be a lot happier. He'd be a lot happier.

He glanced at the old man. "If you were offered the DEVGRU, would you take it?"

Considering, Thomas drained his beer before shaking his head. "Can't say that I would."

"Why not?"

"Because covert ops isn't my passion."

"Does it have to be?"

"For me it does." Thomas faced his son with a direct look. "Your problem is that you're too damned good at too many things, son. You always have been."

Before Mitch could ask what that meant, his father told him.

"When a person is good at one, two things, they tend to naturally find those one or two and focus everything they've got in that direction. It's easy to weed out the stuff that isn't right for them because they simply aren't good at it." He waited for Mitch to nod before continuing. "But some people, they're good at a lot of things. Or at everything. For people like you, weeding out the options comes down to purpose. When you know your purpose, you discard what doesn't fit. Until now, your purpose has always been to advance."

"And now?" Mitch wondered.

"You're choosing a direction. It's one you'll be spending

a lot of your life on. So the question is, what are you passionate enough about to make it your purpose?"

Livi. Her face was the first thing that popped into Mitch's mind. He was definitely passionate about her.

He was passionate about the new training program, about the idea of integrating better methods, of expanding the teams' training. He was inspired by the idea of finding more tools, stronger techniques.

But he wasn't passionate about DEVGRU.

"Grandfather's gonna get his skivvies in a twist again," Mitch reflected.

"Son, I'm of the opinion that how a man handles his skivvies is his own problem." Thomas looked around the seedy bar and grimaced. "What d'ya say we go find a decent restaurant? You can buy me dinner and tell me about this divorcée fitness queen who plays with strippers."

Mitch burst out laughing. Damn, Livi would love that description. Before he could respond, though, his cell phone flashed.

My place, 7:00

Mitch grimaced. "She's pretty pissed at me."

"Wouldn't be surprised. Women have a tendency to get a little tetchy when we screw up."

"Who said I screwed up?" Mitch frowned at his father.

"She's pissed at you, right?"

"Yeah."

"You pissed at her?"

"No," Mitch realized.

"Then you screwed up. If it was mutual, the anger would be mutual. That's how these things work."

Couldn't argue with that. Livi was right—he'd been reacting to the slams to his ego. Not to anything she'd done.

"You're so good at figuring out how things work. Why don't you help me figure out how to fix it?"

"You're gonna have to buy me a steak dinner for that information."

Mitch threw a twenty on the bar and followed his father to the door.

"I'm meeting Livi at seven. But you tell me how to fix things with her and I'll buy you an entire cow."

LIVI PACED FROM one end of her living room to the other. She kicked off her sandals, thinking she could move faster barefoot, and resumed pacing. As soon as she hit that side of the room again she slid her feet back into the sandals, needing the little bit of power those couple of inches offered.

She should have met with Mitch the previous night. She'd told her mother she'd talk to him right away. But she'd gotten home and crawled into bed for that nap Pauline had ordered. And the next thing she knew, it was today. Livi had slept around the clock.

The sleep had done her a world of good. She'd obviously needed it. She'd woken refreshed and, for the first time in weeks, filled with energy.

She should have texted Mitch then, instead of waiting until five. But she'd wanted to work through her own feelings first.

Look at me, putting my needs and wants first.

She paced to the other side of the room, stopping at the table to fiddle with the vase of roses and lilies. She ran her fingers over one of the roses. The rich red petals were still silky soft, the scent heady and romantic.

Livi wanted them to last forever.

She'd wanted that night to last, the light, fun, sexily free relationship with Mitch. Where she didn't have to face choices or make difficult decisions.

She pressed her hand to the flat planes of her stomach,

in awe that there was a tiny life growing inside. That she'd be making huge decisions from now on. Everything from what kind of diapers to buy to which schools to live near.

Livi lifted her chin, straightened her shoulders and realized this was it. Time to adjust her big-girl panties, quit hiding behind her shyness and take control of her life.

Starting with her baby's father.

As she turned to pace again, her hip bumped the table. The vase jostled and one petal fell free. Livi watched it flutter sadly down. Frowning, she looked at the flowers again and saw how many were past their peak. Still lovely, but no longer perfect. Ready to fade and fall away.

That's what she was afraid of with Mitch, she realized.

What they had was so beautiful, filling her senses and her life with pleasure. She loved him beyond words.

But he'd leave.

Whether it was a tour of duty, a mission in a far-off land, or… Livi's throat tightened, terror grabbing at her chest as she finally admitted what she'd skimmed so carefully over before. Or he could die.

Livi stared at the petal until the emotions of that image stopped clawing at her heart. They didn't go away—they simply faded into the background. And they'd always be there, she realized, lifting the petal and rubbing the soft velvet against her lips.

So was her shyness, but she'd learned she could handle that. Not make it go away, but live with it, flourish despite it. It'd be the same with the fear for Mitch's life.

Livi tapped the petal against her cheek and thought of Mitch's advice. What did she need? What did she want?

Him. It was that simple.

Was she going to let fear stop her? Would she hold back because she was worried about how he'd react when she made her demand that they spend the rest of their lives loving each other?

Nope. She was going for it. She believed in miracles now. Who was to say she couldn't have more?

As if it'd been waiting for just that question, the doorbell rang. Deep breath, shoulders back, bright smile.

Time to rock and roll.

But when she pulled open the door and saw Mitch's face, she mostly wanted to cut and run.

He was so gorgeous. Super Hottie, his blue eyes piercing and his perfect smile in place. Suddenly all of the hurt she'd felt at his accusations hit her again. Every doubt, every worry. And she thought she was going to tell this man what she wanted and expect him to simply follow along?

She was an idiot.

"You're so beautiful," Mitch said, his greeting as intense as the look in his eyes. He handed her a rose. Its perfect petals still closed tight, the fragrance filled the entry. Livi's eyes filled with tears. "I'm sorry."

Her gaze flew to his.

"I wanted to tell you that before I came in, so we're not dancing around it," he said with a shrug. "I behaved like an ass the other day. I'm sorry."

Oh. Livi melted. She wanted to throw herself into his arms, declare everything peachy keen and haul him off to bed.

But that wasn't the answer. And he might not even want to be hauled off, stripped naked and seduced.

She looked at the rose again and sighed.

He'd apologized for his behavior. That didn't mean he didn't believe the things he'd said.

"Please, come in." Her smile only trembled a little. "We'll talk."

By the time they crossed the short distance to the couch, Livi's nerves were stretched so tight she had to remind herself to breathe. But it didn't matter how many deep breaths she took—the spots in front of her eyes were still dancing in time with the buzzing in her ears.

Just get it over with, she decided as she sat down.

"There's something I need to tell you," she said, the words coming out in a rush of air.

"Actually, I'd like to have my say first if you don't mind." His face set, Mitch looked like he was about to go into battle. He kept a distance between them when he sat, his body language aloof.

But… She did mind. She had no idea when the best time was to tell a man that oops, he's about to be a father. But the expression on his face was ominous, so she was pretty sure it wasn't right after he ended the relationship.

She couldn't find her voice, and none of the practiced words were coming to mind. So she simply folded her hands in her lap and nodded, hoping she'd figure out how to tell him before he got to good-bye.

"I have strong feelings for you," he said quietly. "Feelings that are at odds with the very specific path I'd planned for my life. Actually, that I'd planned with a great deal of influence from others. But however it came about, my career has always been my highest priority and the idea of asking someone to take a backseat to that priority didn't seem fair."

Livi wanted to tell him that every relationship had elements that weren't fair. But his point was too valid to dismiss that lightly.

"I realized a few things over the last couple of weeks, though," he continued, still using that quiet, unemotional tone. "Looking back, I realize I've fashioned much of my career around what others think. Whenever I reached one of those forks in the road, I asked myself which direction would make me look better. I let that, instead of my own passions, decide my direction."

Livi had thought she loved Mitch with all of her heart.

But hearing that, realizing that he had the same issues she did—albeit on a mountain-to-an-anthill scale—she fell for him even harder.

"If you're looking for someone to condemn that, you're looking at the wrong woman," she said with a soft laugh. "Remember me, always putting others' needs first?"

"Ironic, me lecturing you on that. When it was actually my own dirty little secret," he confessed, reaching over to take her hands in his. "When I always had it, I never had to admit to myself how much I craved that approval, how important it was to me."

"And then I came along," she said quietly. "Me and my videos and my stripper reputation." Tension tightening her limbs, Livi realized how that must have felt.

Mitch's eyes met hers, his gaze both rueful and amused.

"Yep, and then you came along. You forced me to see what mattered. That the only approval I should be chasing is my own." Mitch lifted their hands to his lips, brushing a kiss over her knuckles. "My career matters, Livi. What I do, it is who I am. But that doesn't mean I can't be more. That I can't build a life with someone in addition to having that career."

Livi held her breath, hoping this was going where she thought it was, but afraid to actually believe it.

"I've seen it done. My parents are the perfect example of a military marriage that works." Mitch shifted closer, skimming the back of his hand over her cheek before cupping her chin. "I love you, Livi. I want to build a life with you. I want to support you and cheer you on, to know you're doing the same for me."

"I love you, too," she admitted with a tremulous smile. Mitch leaned forward, halfway in for the kiss, when Livi remembered her promise to herself. "No, wait."

"You changed your mind?" he teased. "You really don't love me?"

"Impossible." Livi gave a watery laugh. "But I do need something from you."

"Anything."

"I need a promise," she said. "I don't have to be the most important thing in your life. I don't want to be your entire focus. What you do, who you are, it makes a difference in the world and we need you."

Mitch's smile was a cute combination of gratitude and male ego.

"But I need you to promise that whatever choices you make today, you won't resent me for them later." She bit her lip until she was sure her voice wouldn't shake. "If you think there's any chance you'll blame me for hindering your career, that you think our being together might become a roadblock for you, I want you to go now. I won't hold it against you."

She'd cry a lot, though. But she'd wait until he was through the door.

"Not going to happen." Mitch adamantly shook his head.

"Good. Because as you told me to do so many times, I'm embracing my emotions and putting my wants and needs first. And if we stay together, if we're going to make this work, I'll be doing just that." *Oh man, here goes.* Livi took a long, deep breath and said in a rush, "After all, I have an example to set for my baby."

"You're an amazing woman, Livi. Strong and sweet and loving. You deserve to get what you want." His smile froze, his eyes going blank with shock. Mitch shook his head as if trying to rearrange his thoughts into something that made sense, then leaned back a little. Not far enough to make her worry he was rejecting her. Just enough for him to study her face.

He opened his mouth, but no words came out so he shook his head again.

"I'm sorry. Could you repeat that?" he finally said after clearing his throat.

"I'm pregnant."

Livi watched his face, desperate for a sign of how he felt about the news. But she couldn't read anything but surprise in his expression.

Was surprise good? Or bad?

"You're going to have my baby?" he clarified slowly. His eyes dropped to her flat stomach. When they lifted again, she nodded. "You're sure?"

He looked as if she'd whacked him upside the head with a barbell. So tense she was afraid she'd explode, Livi nodded again.

Mitch continued to stare. After a few seconds she wondered if maybe she should find a barbell. She had a set of five-pounders in the closet. Then he burst into laughter.

"You're laughing," she said blankly. Of all the reactions she'd imagined, none had included that.

"I don't know anything about kids. Nothing at all about being a father," he explained, sounding delighted. "This is nowhere on the list of approved actions that will further my career."

Her teeth clenched tight, Livi decided to get the ten-pound barbell instead.

"It's perfect," he continued.

"Perfect…?" She pressed two fingers against her temple, wondering if pregnancy was messing with her comprehension. "You're going to be a father. Something you've had no experience with, have never felt any desire *to* experience and that many will say could be detrimental to your career. And you think that's perfect?"

Livi didn't know why she was trying to talk him out of being thrilled with the news, but something was pushing her to make absolutely sure he was truly happy the news.

"Absolutely perfect. I came here to tell you I love you. That I want to build a life together with you," he said, his grin fading into a heartfelt smile. "All this does is make me even more sure that this is perfect. For exactly the reasons you just said. It's not the easy choice. It's not the one that will garner the most kudos. But it feels incredible. It feels right."

And just like that, everything was perfect. Her heart melting at the look in his eyes, Livi finally believed in miracles.

"You've given me everything, Livi. More than I even knew I wanted."

"Everything…?"

Mitch reached out and reverently laid his hand against her stomach where the life they'd created grew. His smile was pure magic as it spread across his gorgeous face.

"Everything."

Epilogue

Labor Day

Mitch Donovan had done a lot of things in his life.

He'd scaled walls and dived to the bottom of the ocean. He'd fought in wars and earned medals. He was a Navy SEAL. The best of the best.

But as he looked in awe at the woman lying on the hospital bed, her temples still beaded with perspiration with her hand tucked in his and a serene smile on her face, he knew the truth.

He had nothing on his wife when it came to heroics.

A couple of nurses bustled in the background, weighing, measuring and cooing. But Mitch only had eyes for Livi.

"That was…" Still in awe, he couldn't seem to find the right words to express how amazing it'd been to watch Livi bring their child into the world.

"That was fast," she said with a laugh. She rubbed her cheek against the back of his hand. "And early. I'm so glad you were able to get back in time."

"Me, too." Instead of being off on some dangerous mission, he'd been just a short flight away at the training center in Nevada.

Yet another reason to be glad he'd chosen to transfer to Coronado and focus on training his fellow SEALs instead of chasing his way further up the ladder.

Lifting Livi's hand to his lips, he rubbed a kiss over her knuckles and considered it the smartest career move he'd made.

Mitch had spent most of his life secretly defining himself by his career, using others people's opinions to gauge whether he was a success or not.

But Livi, at the height of success in her own career, had shown him what really mattered. Instead of putting her fitness videos on hiatus until after the baby was born and then returning to what she knew everyone expected of her, she'd completely revamped Stripped Down Fitness. What had started as an idea for a pregnancy workout video soon turned into a thrice-weekly cable series focusing on The Body Babe's renowned no muss, no fuss style workouts for every woman, at every stage of her life. As soon as she'd come up with the concept, she'd brainstormed with Pauline ways to make it accessible, worked through every challenge, including her own shyness, to launch Stages.

She was amazing.

And she was his.

"Here you go," the nurse said, sliding the bundled blanket into Livi's arms.

Dimly aware of the nurses leaving, Mitch couldn't tear his gaze from Livi's expression as it melted into joy. She lifted tear-filled eyes to his, her face glowing.

"Have you ever seen anyone this gorgeous?" she asked in an awed tone, her finger rubbing over the soft swath of hair on the baby's perfect head.

"Yeah," he said, grinning at her expression as it shifted from shock to challenge.

"You," he said simply.

"Oh." Livi gave him a heart-melting smile. "You're so sweet."

"No. You're the sweet one. I'm lucky."

Mitch looked down at his daughter, humbled by the intensity of his feelings.

So damned lucky.

His father was right.

He might be good at a lot of things, but he was only passionate about a few.

Livi and Morgan topped the list.

He planned to spend the rest of his life showing them.

* * * * *

COMING NEXT MONTH FROM

HARLEQUIN® *Blaze*™

Available February 17, 2015

#835 SEARCH AND SEDUCE
Uniformly Hot!
by Sara Jane Stone
This time, Amy Benton is writing the rules: no strings, no promises and definitely no soldiers. Once she sees gorgeous pararescue jumper Mark Rhodes shirtless, though, she just may break every one...

#836 UNDER THE SURFACE
SEALs of Fortune
by Kira Sinclair
Former SEAL Jackson Duchane is searching for a sunken ship full of gold. Business rival Loralei Lancaster is determined to beat him to it. The race is on—if they can stay out of bed long enough to find the treasure.

#837 ANYWHERE WITH YOU
Made in Montana
by Debbi Rawlins
Stuntman and all-around bad boy Ben Wolf is only visiting Blackfoot Falls for a few days. But Deputy Grace Hendrix makes him want to get in trouble with the law...in a whole new way!

#838 PULLED UNDER
Pleasure Before Business
by Kelli Ireland
When Harper Banks barged into his club, Levi Walsh was ready to dress her down...all the way to her lacy lingerie. Until she tells him she's an IRS investigator—and she's closing his business!

YOU CAN FIND MORE INFORMATION ON UPCOMING HARLEQUIN® TITLES, FREE EXCERPTS AND MORE AT WWW.HARLEQUIN.COM.

HBCNM0215

REQUEST YOUR FREE BOOKS!
2 FREE NOVELS PLUS 2 FREE GIFTS!

HARLEQUIN®

Blaze®

red-hot reads!

YES! Please send me 2 FREE Harlequin® Blaze™ novels and my 2 FREE gifts (gifts are worth about $10). After receiving them, if I don't wish to receive any more books, I can return the shipping statement marked "cancel." If I don't cancel, I will receive 4 brand-new novels every month and be billed just $4.74 per book in the U.S. or $4.96 per book in Canada. That's a savings of at least 14% off the cover price. It's quite a bargain. Shipping and handling is just 50¢ per book in the U.S. and 75¢ per book in Canada.* I understand that accepting the 2 free books and gifts places me under no obligation to buy anything. I can always return a shipment and cancel at any time. Even if I never buy another book, the two free books and gifts are mine to keep forever.

150/350 HDN F4WC

Name	(PLEASE PRINT)

Address	Apt. #

City	State/Prov.	Zip/Postal Code

Signature (if under 18, a parent or guardian must sign)

Mail to the **Harlequin® Reader Service:**
IN U.S.A.: P.O. Box 1867, Buffalo, NY 14240-1867
IN CANADA: P.O. Box 609, Fort Erie, Ontario L2A 5X3

Want to try two free books from another line?
Call 1-800-873-8635 or visit www.ReaderService.com.

* Terms and prices subject to change without notice. Prices do not include applicable taxes. Sales tax applicable in N.Y. Canadian residents will be charged applicable taxes. Offer not valid in Quebec. This offer is limited to one order per household. Not valid for current subscribers to Harlequin Blaze books. All orders subject to credit approval. Credit or debit balances in a customer's account(s) may be offset by any other outstanding balance owed by or to the customer. Please allow 4 to 6 weeks for delivery. Offer available while quantities last.

Your Privacy—The Harlequin® Reader Service is committed to protecting your privacy. Our Privacy Policy is available online at www.ReaderService.com or upon request from the Harlequin Reader Service.

We make a portion of our mailing list available to reputable third parties that offer products we believe may interest you. If you prefer that we not exchange your name with third parties, or if you wish to clarify or modify your communication preferences, please visit us at www.ReaderService.com/consumerschoice or write to us at Harlequin Reader Service Preference Service, P.O. Box 9062, Buffalo, NY 14269. Include your complete name and address.

Mark had been her husband's best friend. Was it wrong to want more from him than a shoulder to cry on?

Read on for a sneak preview of
SEARCH AND SEDUCE,
a UNIFORMLY HOT! novel
by Sara Jane Stone.

"In those first few months, I made a cup of cocoa every night. Then I'd sit here and email you."

"You stopped sending memories of Darren," Mark said. "About six months ago."

"You noticed." Amy lowered the mug, a line of hot chocolate on her upper lip.

His gaze locked on her mouth. He wanted to lean forward and kiss her lips clean.

She shrugged. "I guess I was done living in the past. It was a good idea, though. It helped me find my way through it all."

He stared at their joined hands. "Must have been, if you started a new list."

Her fingers pressed against his skin. "This one's different."

"I know." He felt her drawing closer.

"I'm writing the rules this time." Her eyes lit with excitement. Unable to look away, Mark saw the moment desire rose up to meet her newfound joy.

He withdrew his hand. "I should go."

HBEXP0215

Mark pushed back from the table and stood. But Amy followed, stepping close, invading his space. Her hands rose, and before he could move away, he felt her palms touch his face.

He froze, not daring to move. He didn't even blink, just stared down at her. Her gaze narrowed in on his lips, her body shifting closer. Rising on to her tiptoes, she touched her lips to his.

Mark closed his eyes, his hands forming tight fists at his sides. He felt her tongue touch his lower lip as if asking for more. Unable to hold back, he gave in, opening his mouth to her kiss, deepening it, making it clear that this kiss was not tied to an offering of friendship and comfort.

Amy's hands moved over his jaw, running up through his hair. Pulling his mouth tightly against hers. He groaned. She tasted like chocolate—sweet and delicious. He wanted more, so damn much more.

Her fingers ran down the front of his shirt, moving lower and lower. His body hardened, ready and wanting.

He reached for her wrist, gently drawing her away. Then he leaned closer, his lips touching her ear, allowing her to hear the low growl of need in his voice. "Let me know when you've written your rules."

Don't miss
SEARCH AND SEDUCE by Sara Jane Stone,
available March 2015 wherever
Harlequin® Blaze® books and ebooks are sold.

www.Harlequin.com

Copyright © 2015 by Sarah Tormey

HBEXP0215

Love the Harlequin book you just read?

Your opinion matters.

Review this book on your favorite book site, review site, blog or your own social media properties and share your opinion with other readers!

Be sure to connect with us at:
Harlequin.com/Newsletters
Facebook.com/HarlequinBooks
Twitter.com/HarlequinBooks

HREVIEWS

HARLEQUIN®

A *Romance* FOR EVERY MOOD™

JUST CAN'T GET ENOUGH?

Join our social communities
and talk to us online.

You will have access to the latest
news on upcoming titles and special
promotions, but most importantly,
you can talk to other fans about your
favorite Harlequin reads.

Harlequin.com/Community

 Facebook.com/HarlequinBooks

 Twitter.com/HarlequinBooks

Pinterest.com/HarlequinBooks

HSOCIAL